Run, Rasputin Run!

Trials and Friendships

(Book 2)

by

Jennifer Miller

Illustrated by

Vanessa Knight

Note for Librarians: A cataloguing record for this book is available from Library and Archives Canada at www.collectionscanada.ca/amicus/index-e.html

ISBN 1-4120-8494-6

Printed in Victoria, BC, Canada. Printed on paper with minimum 30% recycled fibre. Trafford's print shop runs on "green energy" from solar, wind and other environmentally-friendly power sources.

Offices in Canada, USA, Ireland and UK

Book sales for North America and international:
Trafford Publishing, 6E–2333 Government St.,
Victoria, BC V8T 4P4 CANADA
phone 250 383 6864 (toll-free 1 888 232 4444)
fax 250 383 6804; email to orders@trafford.com

Book sales in Europe:
Trafford Publishing (UK) Limited, 9 Park End Street, 2nd Floor
Oxford, UK OX1 1HH UNITED KINGDOM
phone 44 (0)1865 722 113 (local rate 0845 230 9601)
facsimile 44 (0)1865 722 868; info.uk@trafford.com
Order online at:
trafford.com/06-0248

10 9 8 7 6 5 4 3 2

CAST of CHARACTERS

Penelope the Duck – Sasha's new friend teaches him how to fish and keeps their secret throughout their long life together: that Sasha, the bear cub, didn't know how.

Mr. Sirus – The crotchety old farmer who shoots at anyone who trespasses on his chicken farm.

Mr. Hare – The squatter on Old Sirus' vegetable garden. Will his secret be found out (stealing all the food he needs to feed his family) or will he go unnoticed and have food aplenty for his family and himself?

Caribou – The healer of the forest inhabitants. Can she save the little cub, Sasha, or will he die from causes unknown?

The Goat Family – who has milk to nurse the wolf pup, Ivanhoe. Will the raccoon be spared from nursing the pup, or will she agree to the command of their healer to feed the whelp?

The Raccoon Family – The mother is called upon to feed the little wolf. She defies the command bitterly, spitting in disgust.

Guinevere the Coyote – Rasputin's Folly. Always fighting Rasputin for her territory – a long past. Will they ever find a solution to their inner battles of attraction for each other?

The Alpha – The leader of a pack that hates the one called Rasputin. Filled with jealousy and rage to destroy him once and for all, to regain his own power and status among the packs, will he succeed in killing his competition or will Rasputin hold the upper paw?

Ivanhoe – Rasputin's latest downfall. Out to seek revenge on the little cub, Sasha, he hunts this night to kill anything that moves on his way to the cub's den. Dragging his catch out into the moonlit night from the brush, he howls in sadness, finding his prize is none other but a baby wolf pup. Will he leave it to die or will he find a way to save his life?

Owls/Foxes/Squirrels & Birds – And all other friends of the forest are part of the family above: playing, mating, and helping one another survive the mean old Rasputin.

This story takes place in the forests of Netherland.

I dedicate my book "Run, Rasputin Run!" to my Mom and Dad with love, appreciation, and precious memories that will last us all a lifetime.

A special tribute to my dear friend, Vivian Dillaway, who enjoyed reading "Run, Rasputin Run" Book 1 from start to finish, and urged me to write Books 2 and 3. You'll always be remembered. We did it!

Contents

Sasha's New Friend   3

The Squatter   15

Sasha Catches his First Fish   25

The Big Celebration   37

Sasha's Illness   53

The Practitioner   63

Rasputin on the Prowl   70

Penelope's Visit to Crotchety Mr. Hare   79

Wolf in the House!   89

Sasha's Past   96

Penelope's Search for Sasha   106

A Visit from Sasha's Ancestors   117

Rasputin's Retribution   127

Rasputin's Story   138

A Cry for Help   146

The Pact   153

Author's Words   **165**

Sasha's New Friend

Sasha ran throughout the forest, happy he had a new home and new friends. On and on he raced, stopping from time to time, discovering new wonders of this land. His eyes caught sight of a bubbling stream up ahead.

Water meant fish!

He leaped with playful abandon. Running around in circles, he chased a colorful butterfly that hovered over his head, as if asking for some playtime. Sasha reared up, pawing at the

branch it landed on, then chased after it as it flew off – teasing this clumsy cub with antics known only to creatures in flight.

Remembering the stream that promised him a hearty meal, he gave

up the chase, ambling off towards the stream and leaving the butterfly to find someone else to play with. He jumped into the water, splashing wildly about, scaring away all the fish. Paws splashed in and out of the stream, making loud spattering sounds.

A lone duck watched this display with disgust, not believing her eyes. Didn't this obnoxious bear know how to fish? It was scaring away all the bugs she had been trying to catch, which had been swimming around closer and closer to her, almost within reach.

Sasha, unaware of being watched, jumped off a large rock, belly-flopping back into the water. He swam around happily, diving underneath, trying to catch his meal. Not seeing any fish, he swam to the top, shaking his head to clear his eyesight. With a loud bellow, he lazily rolled over on his back, sunning himself and letting the steam carry him slowly with the current towards the duck, who really didn't want him to interrupt her time here anymore then it already was. She eyed him dispassionately as he drew closer, eyes closed and half asleep.

Quacking loudly, she fluffed out her feathers, watching her meal drift off in another area.

"You there!" she called. "Can't you go someplace else to play? Twice you have chased my lunch away!"

Sasha opened his eyes quickly, not too happy about being wakened from his dreamy state. He stared into the hostile eyes of the duck and wondered who this noisy pest was. He rolled over on his belly to have a better look, sizing up the situation in no time at all.

"Oh, hi!"

He splashed the water with joy, happy he had found a new companion on this outing.

"Oh hi yourself!" The duck stormed. "Didn't anyone ever teach you how to fish?"

"I know how to fish," answered the little cub, not sure if he wanted this complaining fowl to be his companion after all. He shook out his fur again, sending spray all over the freshly bathed duck. Seeing her eyes full of fury, he kicked himself over on his belly, trying to get as far away from this unfriendly foe as fast as he could.

"Now look at what you've done!" She swam after this oaf, coming alongside of him. "I started to have a peaceful morning, and waiting patiently for my meal, then you come thrashing into the water!"

"I don't know what I have done, but you are angry with me, and–"

"You don't know what you've done? LOOK AT ME!" she stormed. "I am FILTHY!"

Sasha wearily opened his eyes, wishing he had chosen another place now than here, to do his discovering. He took in the sight of this noisemaker. She did look a bit ... disheveled.

"Well?" The duck swam closer, eyeing this clumsy ball of fur angrily.

"Your wings will dry, and once this is done, you can bathe yourself ..."

"I already bathed myself! I almost had my meal to fill this empty belly of mine, and I was doing just fine, until you ruined my morning!"

Sasha sighed, "I will catch you a fish."

"You?" sputtered the duck. "I just witnessed *your* fishing skills."

Sasha shrugged his shoulders, water splashing back up on the duck.

"Sorry," he mumbled.

The duck gave a few angry sounds in farewell and sadly swam off.

"Wait!"

Sasha swam after her.

"Go away. I need to get my meal and take some food back to my hungry family."

Sasha swam silently with the duck, carefully keeping his splashings as still as possible. He watched her tail make quick swishing movements from side to side, trying to out-swim him, her head making darting looks, searching for her meal. Seeing some bugs floating ahead he kept back, letting her make her catch. He watched tail feathers go bottoms-up as she dove underneath the surface.

Sasha waited.

Sasha waited some more.

Then, being worried, he dove underneath himself, trying to catch sight of the duck, who was probably in trouble and needed his help. He caught sight of her, beak filled with bugs and moss.

Then the duck spotted him.

She glared at him beneath the water, swimming back to the top – where she bumped into him – his eyes filled with regret and embarrassment.

"I'm sorry."

The duck held on to her catch, fearful she would lose her meal if she spoke her mind. Turning on her belly, she headed home, happy to be gone from her troublemaker.

Sasha watched her swim away. At least she had her meal. Maybe they would meet again and he could make a better impression. Was she ever in a good mood? He wondered what made her so grumpy.

Hearing loud noises overhead, he spotted a couple gulls.

"Oh-oh."

Seeing them circle the duck, he paddled as fast as he could towards his companion, hoping to get to her in time ... before the gulls got to her. They could be mean, and during the course of stealing her food, could hurt her in the struggle.

He sighed. This was not the morning he had planned on having.

He glanced nervously up at the circling gulls, hoping he could reach the duck before they attacked. He paddled faster, almost catching up to her; and hearing the cub coming up to her, she hurried on.

"Wait!" Sasha called. "You're in trouble!"

She paddled faster, a tight hold on her food in her beak.

"I am coming to you for fear the gulls will steal your food, and in the process, may injure you. If you slow down, I will swim with you until you are safely back to your nest."

The gulls swooped down on the duck, skimming the water in front of her, trying to grab her food. Sasha splashed his paw at them, frightening them off; then down they dove again, this time coming closer, grabbing for her food, and taking flight again – not giving up their pursuit.

The duck swam faster, looking sideways at Sasha, eyes meeting his with a little more warmth than before.

Cries of more gulls filled the air. Down they all dove, straight towards the duck again.

"Dive!" Sasha yelled. "I'll take care of these once and for all!"

Bottoms-up went the duck again, just in time before the gulls attacked her. Hanging on to her food to take back to her little ones at home, she dove deeper, hearing all the commotion above. Sasha splashed angrily at the gulls to chase them off, but they kept flying up, diving at Sasha who had chased their duck away.

Sasha bellowed loudly, feeling the bite of several of them. He swiftly rolled over on his back, splashing with all fours, kicking water heavily at the approaching gulls and wishing some of his friends were here to help out. They'd know what to do, and right now, he wasn't sure how to scare away these pests.

Another bellow sounded, and Sasha fought them unsuccessfully. The duck suddenly appeared beside him, all food gone, and eyes filled with fury. She bit into one of the advancing gulls and feathers went flying through the air. Others came diving at her and she took flight, circling around them, nipping at their sides and beaks.

She fought bravely, taking a few bites from the angry gulls. Sasha continued splashing the water to try to divert their attention. Finally they gave up, screeching off into the brush, happy to leave those two alone.

Sasha swam to the duck.

"Thanks. I wasn't sure how to fight those nasty birds." He looked closer, seeing blood ooze from her foot. "You're hurt. And you lost your food. I am sorry," he mumbled.

The duck eyed him gently. "You are hurt too. Those gulls are mean ... your paw needs fixing."

Sasha looked down at his paw. The pad was cut and he wriggled his foot.

"My foot moves," he grinned. "I'm alright, but you are without food for your family. LOOK!"

He pointed to a circle of bugs and water cattails, sticking up from the marsh.

"I know! I will dive, swoop all the bugs and some vegetation off onto my back, and when I surface, we'll swim together back to your nest, and you take your meal off my back!"

The duck eyes Sasha intently, knowing he was trying to help. She fluttered her wings gently.

"Alright. Then follow me back to my nest; and once my family is fed, I'll wrap some aloe weed around your paw. That's a great remedy, and you will stay and eat with us."

Sasha didn't reply.

"We'll both dive for clams and fish. You'll have a great feast."

Sasha bellowed happily. "Let's go! First we get the food for your family, and then off we go to your nest."

They smiled, both happy and at last, friends. Sasha was already tasting his clams. If he was lucky, a big fish too! He was very hungry.

The Squatter

Old Hare rabbit walked angrily throughout his garden, hands thrust deep in his tattered pockets, mouth uttering angry complaints against his new neighbors who had settled in this last spring. No sooner had they made themselves at home, which was bad enough, but they were helping themselves to his garden.

He looked around as he walked up and down each row, eyeing the heavy damage. He picked up a carrot lying on the ground, half eaten, then discarded.

"Dang it!"

If they were going to steal from him, at least they could eat all of their food, he scowled. He eyed the flattened crop where they bed down each night, in the safety of his garden.

Everyone feared the mean old Rasputin, seen all too many a time in these parts. No doubt they were hiding from him, but must they choose *his* garden to hide in? He kicked a fallen ear of corn out of his path.

"DANG!" he repeated.

He was starting to acquire a taste for corn – a nice change from all those carrots. He looked out across his large garden. It took a long time to harvest his crop. Maybe the Mrs. could put some in jars, like he saw the two-legged neighbors a half month ago do, as he was preparing to steal some seed from their shed.

He chuckled, remembering that night. The Mrs. had made him a hat to keep him warm on those cold blustering nights. He turned it inside-out and loaded seed from the old farmer's bin. It worked just fine, and held a lot of seed, but it stretched some – and when he hurried back to his lair he emptied all the seed from his prized gift, and putting his hat back on his head, before entering his home, it was so big it fell down over his mouth.

Loosing his footing from eyes covered, he rolled down the hole smack in front of the Mrs. Well, it was just bad luck that's all, and he tried to explain that the seed would be their food this harsh winter and their young-uns would never go hungry. That helped ... some.

He chuckled, then, spotting Heathcliff, scowled a greeting.

"What are you doing in these parts, Heathcliff?"

"Hi there, Mr. Hare. I brought over some berries I know Mrs. Hare likes."

The old hare looked intently at Heathcliff, wondering what that thing was he was carrying on his back. Heathcliff shifted his weight, bringing the pack to the ground with a thud.

"This is something Mr. Mouse and I invented. Great idea, don't you think?"

"Hmmp. I guess so."

"We found a whole patch full of these. Let me know if you want some more!"

"What else is inside? That's a pretty heavy thing, for just carrying berries."

"Oh, I almost forgot! Some moss for your beds. It's nice and soft, and keeps you warm at night when the winter comes."

"Hmmp. That's a lot of trouble for you to go through just for my family."

"Oh! Mr. Mouse helped with all this ... in fact, most of it. He chose me to carry it, as I am more able than he in these matters."

"What do you want for all your trouble?" the old hare asked, face full of suspicion.

"Nothing," smiled Heathcliff. "Well, I must be off. Give my regards to your family."

Heathcliff hopped off, leaving the crotchety old hare embarrassed with his manners. "Hey Heathcliff!" he called after the visitor.

Heathcliff stopped, turning back towards Mr. Hare.

"I heard you have a bear living with you. Is this true?"

"Oh, you are referring to Sasha! A bear cub, which got himself in some trouble a few months back."

"The same," Mr. Hare grumbled. "Old Rasputin almost had him for dinner, the story goes, when your Mr. Mouse helped him to safety. Darnest story I ever heard of. Any of it true?"

"Oh yes!" Heathcliff happily replied. "All of it. Why you wouldn't believe the whole story! Why let me tell you –"

"Another time Heathcliff, Mr. Hare muttered. I must get back to weeding out the damage those nasty deer are doing to my garden.

"Deer, you say?" grinned Heathcliff. "Probably after some seed you took from Old Sirus, the farmer."

"Watch your manners, you little wippersnit!" scolded the hare.

"Your secret is safe!" laughed Heathcliff.

"How do you know these stories?"

Heathcliff tugged at his ear. Mr.Mouse saw you one night, as the moon was going down.

"Hmmp! What was he doing out there? That's a long way from these parts. Well, never mind. You best be on your way ... and thanks from the Mrs. for the moss and berries."

Heathcliff chuckled. Waving happily, he raced off. He had a full night ahead of him, as Sasha and Mr. Mouse had a surprise for him. He wondered what it was.

He dashed off into the brush, keeping himself concealed as much as possible. The sun was going down, and dusk was setting in.

Must hurry, he thought.

He wasn't in the mood to outrun old Rasputin this night. He was just too happy.

••

Now spring had set in, and all the forest was filled with love and gaiety. Flowers bloomed with beauty, their bright colors shining proudly through the pines, fragrances floating throughout the land. It was a time of mating and rebirth. Nests and lairs were being built or added on to, making room for new additions to their expectant families.

Every living creature of the forest wove garlands together, each bringing their friends and neighbors some extra peat moss. Berries were mixed with vegetation of every kind available throughout the land, to help out with the food supply before the heavy snowfalls of winter came upon them. It was a glorious time, when all helped the other with the building and preparation of having enough food and warmth throughout the season ahead.

The evenings soft moon glow brought them all together, socializing and telling tales way into the night while the young slept on, in the comfort of their warm beds nearby. Events were caught up on, things that happened in the absence of the other

– one such story was of how Sasha came to be a new friend to them all; how Mr. Mouse had been so brave as to get as close to old Rasputin's ear and bite it as hard as he could, to help save Sasha, the little cub.

Contests were planned, fairs and the ball of the season was the talk of the forest – its main festivity. It was the time for introductions, courtship, and mating.

Ah, spring had sprung!

■■■

From time to time, old Rasputin was spotted prowling the highlands and flatlands, searching for anything he could chase down and eat, hungry or not. He was still licking his wounds from that unforgettable night the troublesome owls bested him. He howled half into the night, weeks on end, since that fateful event ... promising each of them revenge! Why, even in his sleep he would jump wide awake from tormenting dreams, cold and shaking with anger.

He would get even with them all! Especially that furball of a bear cub.

How was it, he wondered throughout his days and nights, he was fighting a cub one minute, then the next before the hopeful kill – a grizzly. His mind had to be playing tricks on him.

He often thought he had been more weary and hungry than he thought. That *had* to have been it. No one outsmarted, outran, or outhunted Rasputin! He would plan his hunt, each one individually, and rid the forest of such scum once and for all! Yes Siree!

It was these thoughts that kept old Rasputin going.

Cocky and more arrogant than ever, he tormented all within his sight, howling gleefully day and night to send terror throughout the land.

Sasha Catches his First Fish

"Now first of all, let me teach you how to fish. How is it that you, a bear, small as you are and all, doesn't know how to fish?" The duck looked at Sasha intently.

Sasha swam slowly beside his newfound friend. He glanced sideways as if to answer, then decided not to.

"Well, never mind," snapped the duck. "If you don't want to tell me, don't. But I just think it strange that you are running around all alone in such a dangerous area, with no one to watch over you."

Sasha gulped, then hurried ahead, looking for some food to feed this chatterbox and its family.

"Of course if you are older than you appear to be, then I guess that's the reason why you are out running about, scaring away all the fish from those who are hungry and have a family to feed," quipped the duck.

Sasha turned over on his back, splashing water up on the indignant duck.

"Well I never!"

She fluffed her wings out and stared at this pest in front of her.

"Sorry," mumbled Sasha, not knowing what else to say.

They both swam together, quietly as a leaf floating ahead of them.

"My ancestors were shot by poachers. I was too young to be taught how to fish, or other ways of the bear."

"Well why didn't you say so! Would have saved me a lot of talking. Have you no friends?" asked the concerned duck.

"Oh yes!" Sasha happily replied. "Do you know Heathcliff and Mr.Mouse?"

"I do."

"Well, one night Rasputin almost had me for dinner along with Mr. Mouse."

"I heard tell of that story. So, *you* are Sasha! Well, I

never ... "

"You heard of the story?" asked Sasha, happy he had finally broken the barrier of communication with this one.

"Everyone around these parts has heard tell of that story many times. Aren't you afraid of being all alone out here?" asked the duck.

"Well, sometimes ... but I thought I would come here alone, and learn how to fish, before all my friends find out I don't know how."

Embarrassed, he turned over on his belly and continued to swim.

The duck was touched by his story. Sighing, she swam faster to catch up. She splashed water up on Sasha, who turned sideways – surprised.

The duck smiled.

"Now we are even."

Both smiled happily. They continued to swim, looking for some food.

"I will teach you how to fish, Sasha. It will be our secret. When you see your friends again, you will be a bear who knows how to catch large fish – and not frighten them away!

First, you must be closer to the shoreline; second, next to a waterfall ... fish love to swim up river or stream; third, bears love to catch darting fish as they jump out of the water, heading up stream.

Bears are swift, and their long claws on the front feet make it very easy to catch fish. What else do you eat?"

"Berries and roots, eggs from abandoned nests, and sometimes my friends come across a carcass and I eat some of the remains and bone marrow.

"Have you ever had fish?" the duck asked.

"Not yet," Sasha admitted shyly.

"Well, let's go get you some fish ... as soon as I feed my fledglings, that is. They are no doubt making a lot of noise back at the nest, and screaming for their dinner."

The duck dove underneath the water, swiftly resurfacing with a mouth full of food.

"How did you do that?" asked the cub, surprised and pride showing in his eyes.

Not answering, the duck happily swam towards her nest, Sasha following close behind. He was happy the duck's family was about to be fed, and knowing that soon ... he was going fishing!

●●●

Heathcliff raced through the brush, hoping to be back before Sasha arrived back to the lair. Lately the cub went out a lot by himself. He wondered where he went but knew that when the time was right, the little bear would confide in him.

Mr. Mouse was concerned too, but didn't want to pry. Maybe he just needed to find some time to be alone and sort a lot of things out. It wasn't easy being an orphan ... then almost being eaten up by old Rasputin and in the jaws of death had been hard on him too.

Heathcliff stopped and looked around, scratching his long ear as he liked to do when deep in thought. He pondered, watching the sun set. He knew Sasha was happy having his new friends. He had a warm den and lots of food.

FOOD.

Heathcliff frowned. Maybe the little bear needed more. Sasha was very young, he knew this; he guessed maybe not even a year old yet. Bears usually stayed with the females until two, then left their den, going out on their own in search of a mate and planning a family of their own.

Sasha didn't speak much of his ancestors ... only that from time to time they would appear and speak to him. This puzzled all of them, as they never saw Sasha's ancestors. Was he saying this because he was lonely? Or had he really been visited by them?

Heathcliff started on his journey once more, wanting to be back at the lair before Sasha returned.

He watched each morning at early daybreak, before darkness left, and saw Sasha leave the den morning after morning, not saying a word and going as silently as he could, glancing back from time to time, leaving the area. Was he afraid of being seen leaving? Why? They were all friends. What was going on?

Well, never mind, Heathcliff thought. In time Sasha would open up. He was still new to all this, and although he seemed content and happy, Heathcliff was certain the little bear had some things to work out. He would just have to be patient – all of them; in the meantime they would watch over him, without being noticed, to give the little bear alone time to work out whatever it was he needed to.

···

"No! No! No!" admonished the duck. "You can't jump in the water like a clumsy oaf! You keep scaring away the fish!"

Sasha looked impatient at the fish jumping out of the water, as if making fun of the little bear's poor fishing skills.

"Fishing requires great knowledge and tenacity," the duck said. "Great knowledge and tenacity ... and patience. These

things you don't have."

Sasha looked sad.

"Yet," the duck smiled, "you will. I will teach you to be the best fish catcher in these parts, but you must follow my instructions.

Hour after hour, day after day way into the evening, Sasha continued to leave his den at early morn, before the sun came up, and saunter quietly through the forest to meet the duck in the same stream they had met weeks ago.

Time was running out, as soon the planned ball was approaching, and there were all kinds of contests and events to enter. He wanted to enter the fishing contest and couldn't let his friends know he didn't know how to catch a fish. He was their hero. How would they feel if they found out? This worried the little bear so much that half the night he would lie awake, going over in his head the lessons from the day on how to catch a fish. He no sooner fell asleep then it was time to rise and shine, and saunter off to meet the duck.

Each day he promised to ask her name, but once in the water, and starting another day of 'How to Catch a Fish,' he was so weary before hurrying back to his friends that he forgot to ask.

Then one day it happened ...

Sasha caught his first fish!

"Hang on to it!" screamed the duck. "Don't let it get away!"

Flapping her wings against the water, she was ecstatic.

"Hang on! It's a beauty! Don't let go! Sasha, you caught your first fish!"

She flew up out of the water, circling him, quacking loudly and full of excitement. Sasha, who towered high above the water himself – a big smile on his face – hung on so tight to the large speckled trout that it slid out of his paw and went diving back towards the water.

The duck screamed a warning, but too late. She flew – catching the frantic fish with her beak, and in one movement, tossed it back up towards the shocked little bear, who still hadn't had the time to feel the disappointment of losing his

trout. In one split second he gained his wits and, seeing his fish being tossed back to him, thrust out his paw, catching the fish in mid air.

Seeing the happy expression of the duck at his victory, he hung on tightly to the trout, letting out a triumphant roar that shook the forest. At last he was a bear! He rocked from side to side, victorious and filled with pride.

"You did it!" squealed the happy duck. "You caught a fish! A large speckled trout that a grizzly would be proud of claiming, Sasha; YOU DID IT!"

Sasha roared loudly once more, fish raised to the heavens above, as if showing off his trophy. He jumped off the rock he was on, hanging on firmly to his prize – he held it secured in his mouth – swimming towards the duck, splashing happily.

Duck and bear splashed one another with joy, knowing now that Sasha's worries were over. Once reaching shore, Sasha looked hesitantly at the duck, swaying side to side.

"Go Sasha, go on back to your friends with your catch. Come back when you're wanting to fish and I'll be here. Go."

Sasha bellowed once more, circling in a playful strut, then racing off towards home, happy and victorious.

The duck watched with pride and friendship. Today she knew she had found a new friend, and it was just the beginning of many good times fishing together.

She dove beneath, looking for food for her family. Happily, she swam back towards her nest, splashing water more than usual ... remembering Sasha's splatterings with her. The sun was going down. A soft breeze started to roll across the water, the distant croaking of frogs bringing the close to a delightful day.

The Big Celebration

"I don't know," Heathcliff sadly replied. "All I do know is he leaves here before the sun comes up, arriving back looking sad and very distraught."

Mr. Mouse tapped his foot nervously, as he always did when he had a lot on his mind. "Maybe he's pondering which contest to enter at the fair. I think, knowing Sasha, he wants to surprise us.

"You don't believe that!" Mr. Possum encircled his body with his long tail. "I am worried about him."

The howl of Rasputin broke the solemn moment, as they all jumped in fright.

Mr. Mouse let out a squeal of horror, "That's old Rasputin! Do you think he's after Sasha?" He jumped up, pacing back and forth, looking around with fear. "Come on! We've got to find him before its too late!"

A loud thrashing in the brush had them all jumping for cover, eyes wide with fright, teeth chattering while all was as still as the moon breaking through the clouds.

Out raced Sasha, eyes full of excitement, holding the largest fish they had ever seen. They watched in awe, feelings mixed with respect and relief. Still in hiding, unable to move, they watched their little friend roar loudly, rearing high up – trying to touch the sky – fish flapping back and forth in wild abandon. Then the little bear ran in circles, throwing dust up in the faces of those who watched. He threw himself upon the ground, pawing at the trees overhead, happy and the victor.

Mr. Mouse sneezed from all the dust.

Sasha jumped back to his standing position, walking happily towards the brush, recognizing Mr. Mouse.

Mr. Mouse sneezed again, "Sasha! Where have you been? We were all so worried that something had happened to you!"

Sasha looked around at all his friends, still hanging firmly on to his fish. Swaying from side to side, he walked over to Heathcliff, then back to Mr. Mouse. He eyed the little tyrant, and then dropped his prized fish in front of him. Mr. Mouse jumped back, not taking his eyes off the large trout.

"I went fishing," Sasha laughed. "I caught the biggest one in the stream. I had a few smaller ones, but I threw them back!" He bellowed loudly, happy and proud.

Mr. Possum, Heathcliff, and Mr. Mouse all gazed at their friend with admiration and wonder. Mr. Possum stepped hesitantly forward, gazing up at the little bear.

"But where have you been going every morning before the sun came up?"

Sasha roared happily, "I have been fishing! Each morning I would go to the stream towards Mr. Hare's place. There's a roaring stream where all the fish jump in and out, going up stream.

"But ... but how did you know how to fish," the little possum stammered, "you but a wee cub?"

"Ah!" laughed Sasha. "It was difficult, but bears have a natural-born talent to fish! I tried to choose the big trout, but throwing back the smaller ones took me more time than I hoped."

"Did you see mean old Mr. Hare?" asked Heathcliff.

"Nope! I had only one thing in mind – to catch me the largest fish seen in these parts – ever!" Sasha roared with joy, strutting around like it was a grand day for celebration.

Heathcliff eyed him with suspicion. Now he knew he was out at old Mr. Hares,' and narry a sight of this little storyteller. Sasha appeared too happy with himself though; he decided not to say anything, so let it go. Another time when the two were alone. He didn't want to pry but he had to let Sasha know that telling stories and being the hero was all right, but to also tell him that they liked him the way he was, and he didn't have to make up all these outrageous stories to be accepted as one of them.

Sasha was demonstrating how he jumped up on the rocks and dove in, catching the fish as they swam happily about. His paws reached out, grabbing the air, showing everyone staring at him with reverence.

"I lost this one, Mr. Mouse, as I got careless in hanging on to him. One must never get careless! He slipped through my paw, and ... guess what? Before he hit the water I reached out and caught him the second time!"

Sasha bellowed, strutting about proudly, walking in front of Heathcliff now. Eyes met. Heathcliff scratched his long ear sadly.

Sasha swayed slowly from side to side, feeling embarrassed, knowing Heathcliff didn't believe his story. Everyone looked on, wondering why the sudden change in mood.

"Sasha!" Heathcliff exclaimed. "You are truly the hero this night. Let's prepare a celebration!"

Everyone cheered, happy for any excuse to have some celebration! It was spring! Heathcliff smiled at Sasha.

"You are a fine catcher of fish! Now, please tell us more of your adventurous day while we prepare for the night's festivities!"

Sasha leaped over to where his fish lie and happily grabbed it up, running to and fro to help in any way he could, his prize flapping from side to side in all the excitement. He stayed close to Heathcliff, hoping he wouldn't say anything to the others about his false story.

Now, old Raputin knew something was going on with all the furballs because there was a lot of noise and constant chatter going on night after night. Well, he would just have to saunter on over there where all the racket was and have a look. The night was young and he was hungry!

He climbed the highest point where he usually did, trying to spot his prey out roaming about. He sniffed the air, trying to pick up any unusual scent. He spotted old Hare's place off in the far distance to the north of him. He knew there was a family of deer living in those parts, but he felt the sting of those hooves too many times to be foolish enough to try again. He'd wait until they had their young, then plan his kill.

He studied the stream that flowed through the valley behind old Hare's place. Tomorrow he'd check out that area. He thought he had spotted a mangy little bear there, but he knew the one he almost had for dinner a while back had probably been too scared to venture out on his own again.

He licked his chops, getting crazy with all his dreams of getting even! He'd find that deranged vermin and tear him apart limb by limb, oh yes siree! He wouldn't get a good night's sleep until he had his revenge. His eyes narrowed into tiny slits as he relived that night they all bested him. He'd kill them all!

Feeling victorious he raised his large head, letting a piercing howl fill the forest. Until he spotted his bunch of flea-bags, he would torment his victims. He knew everyone feared old Rasputin!

He chuckled as he started his descent down the side of the mountain. One thing he was sure of ... the mangy little bear was loosing his senses. He snickered, remembering how he kept talking to himself down the well, seeing things that weren't there. He kept talking to his ancestors as if they would come back from the dead and help him. Bringing that little furball down would not only be a game of fun, but an easy one besides.

Old Rasputin took off on a run, feeling the best he had in a long time. Spotting a prairie dog, he raced faster, knowing soon he would have his dinner.

Life was good, yes siree!

What a feast it was! The ground was covered with berries, nuts, fruit, carrots, peat moss, cheese, and last but not least – fish, spread neatly upon the berries. They all sat around telling tales and filling their stomachs so full they could hardly move. Half of Sasha's large trout was already devoured, except for the tail he displayed proudly on top of the berries. His trophy shone with pride and joy.

Each talked of the upcoming contests they held each year before the ball. Mr. Possum, happy to be reunited with his family after the rescue of Sasha, Mr. Mouse, and himself, chewed on a nut, wondering what he could do if he entered. At last he looked over at Mr. Mouse.

"What are you going to enter, Mr. Mouse?" he asked. "What special skills do you have?"

Sasha bellowed enthusiastically, "Biting Rasputin's Ear!"

Mr.Owl flew over on a limb, joining the festivities of the night; Daisy close behind. Mr. Owl spoke firmly but with humor, "Not one I think he wants to repeat!"

"Well I certainly hope not!" chimed in Daisy, sitting closer to her mate, wings touching him lovingly. "One night such as that one is enough for one lifetime!" Clicking her beak in admonishment, she eyed the group below her.

All the animals looked up, happy to see them. Heathcliff hopped closer to the tree they both landed on.

"Hi there! How did you find us?"

"Well, all the chatter and excitement reached our ears, so we thought we would fly over and see what's up," Daisy answered. "Looks like a celebration."

Mr. Owl spoke hesitantly, "I think our little Sasha here caught himself a prize, that right?" He looked down intently at the little cub.

"How did you know this?" Sasha asked, eyes wide and excited.

"Oh, we owls see many things, night after night."

Sasha gulped shyly, "Did you see me catch my fish?"

"I did."

"You ... you did?" The little bear looked down, rubbing his back against the tree.

"Yes! And my eyes shone with pride!" Mr. Owl remarked, looking intently at the little cub. "Sometimes the catch is not the important part, but the time and learning about catching the fish ... now that's the vital part. You never gave up, and you learned a great deal these past nights. For that I am proud of you, little bear; but it was unwise to go off by yourself. Next time take one of your friends, who know these parts better than you. That way you have put your trust in them, and therefore a friendship becomes stronger."

Heathcliff glanced up at Mr. Owl, and Mr. Owl winked back at Heathcliff, then nudged Daisy, "You ready for more flying?"

"I most certainly am! I think I have heard enough about fishing and men talk. Yes. I am ready."

She smiled down at all the creatures below, understanding all too well what Mr. Owl was talking about, for she had been there watching Sasha and the duck far to long. Now she wanted to get back to their favorite past time – flying, and rebuilding their nest. Lord knows she needed a larger one, with young ones coming soon.

Smiling happily she looked down at Sasha, "You are still very young. Don't go wandering off by yourself anymore. We are all friends here.

Anything you need to learn or know about, who better to tell you but us?" Clicking her beak softly, she flew off the branch in pursuit of her mate.

Mr. Possum looked back at Mr. Mouse.

"Let me answer your question," replied the mouse. "I am going to enter the flying event."

"But you can't fly."

"Ah! Oh yes I can," chuckled Mr. Mouse.

"But how? You don't have wings!" Mr. Possum reluctantly answered.

"Now let me think," answered the little mouse. "I can fly eight feet into the air; and before I land, can do four somersaults! Boomedy Boom! Boomedy Boom! Boomedy Boom!"

They all laughed, feeling too full and foolish!

"And that's not all!" Mr. Mouse laughed. "My tail acts like a rudder when sailing through the air. At the end of my tail here," he happily demonstrated by pulling his long tail around to his chest, "is a brush at the end I use for balance and scraping the ground, looking for dried seeds and plant stems."

Heathcliff chuckled, "I have seen him fly! That's how he wins so many races!"

Mr. Mouse interrupted, stroking his tail and laughing, "No. I win all my races with you on all fours, on the ground. You're just too slow, Heathcliff, to catch me!"

On and on they teased one another, planning for the big event of outrunning, outflying, and competing against the other, honing their skills and the different talents each one had.

Still tugging at his tail, Mr. Mouse looked over at his friend, Heathcliff.

"Speaking of flying, I heard you flew on the back of Mr. Owl. What a sight *that* must have been!"

"One I don't care to repeat either," answered Heathcliff, grinning. "Which brings to mind old Rasputin! He has been seen many a time out stalking the flatlands, looking for us. I want all of us to take extra precaution. And you, Sasha, will be the first one he'll want to destroy. You bested him, and he won't ever live it down until he gets his revenge."

"But look how many fish he caught!" the possum exclaimed. "Sasha is so brave!"

Cheers went up. Sasha glanced at Heathcliff, eyes wide with apprehension.

"Yes," Heathcliff answered, "like Mr. Owl said, but remember we are all friends here. We can help each other. You're right, Mr. Possum, Sasha is very brave, and he brought back his large fish to share with us ... but he must take more precautions in the future, and understand he is one of us now; and although fishing and storytelling are his two strongest traits now, he must understand he doesn't always have to be the hero for us to like him more than we already do."

Heathcliff made eye contact with the embarrassed Sasha and continued ...

"Liking you more then we already do isn't possible. We made you a part of our family for your goodness, not your skills."

Sasha bellowed softly, saying he wanted to change the subject. He wished no more of his scoldings. He clumsily patted the tail of his fish, feeling uncomfortable.

"Now!" Heathcliff laughed, seeing the little bear's embarrassment, "Let's talk more of the contest." His eyes shifted to the family of deer lying close by, chewing on some mistletoe. "Let's talk of your skills for the competition."

Off in the distance a lone wolf's angry howl was heard throughout the forest.

Sasha's Illness

"I can't wake him!" Mr. Mouse cried. He kept pinching Sasha's nose.

"What is all the commotion?" Heathcliff called, jumping out of his lair. "What is all the noise so early in the morning?"

"Heathcliff! Come quickly! Sasha won't wake up!"

Heathcliff raced over to where Mr. Mouse was – on top of Sasha – pinching the little bear's nose.

Sasha lay still, hardly breathing.

Heathcliff saw Mr. Mouse all in a tether, and fear in his eyes.

"What happened?" he cried.

"I don't know! I woke up, seeing if he had gone off early again, as he had been doing, and he just laid there. I got scared and kept trying to wake him, but it didn't work. Heathcliff! Sasha is dead!"

"Now, now, Sasha can't be dead. But if you don't stop pinching his nose he may very well be so in a bit."

Heathcliff hopped up on the branch lying beside the little bear. He gazed into his face, quiet and soaking wet.

"Um ..." he whispered.

"What's wrong with him!" cried Mr. Mouse, eyes wide and pacing to and fro – as he had a habit of doing when frightened.

"I'm not sure. We must get help. Sound the alarm."

Mr. Mouse raced off, waking everyone and scurrying to the tall tree where nuts of every kind were hung on a vine against a large boulder with an old cow bell, stolen from the farmer's place. He tugged on the vine, sending the warning throughout the land that trouble was here and help was needed.

The high-pitched sound of the bell carried throughout the forest, waking everyone who still slept from the long night before. Mr. Owl, barely asleep, was awakened sharply. Daisy opened her large eyes, looking towards her mate.

"That's the warning bell!" she exclaimed.

"Now calm down Daisy, and go back to sleep. I'll call the code of the forest, when there's trouble, but that's all we can do. It's daylight and we can't see to help."

Mr. Owl let out three piercing shrills of the owl, waking all others up. Each one would repeat the three calls of the owls and wake the whole forest to the warning, each territory spreading the alarm.

"What can it be for?" Daisy asked.

"I don't know," Mr. Owl sadly replied. "But let's not go

jumping to conclusions! We all stayed up late, and maybe they just over-ate too many berries, or ate too much fish!"

"Fish indeed!" Daisy snorted. "I don't believe that, and neither do you!"

Both were silent, hunched close together on their limb.

"Mr. Owl?"

"Yes Daisy?"

"Do you think Rasputin got hold of one of them?"

"One of them?" Mr. Owl frowned. "Let's hope not."

"If he were to attack it would be the little bear first," Daisy sadly whispered.

"You're probably right, but don't worry until we know for sure what's going on."

"Well! We can't just sit here out on a limb and not do anything!"

"Daisy, there is nothing we can do in the daytime. You know this as well as I do. All we can do is keep sounding the alarm, which we will do until we get the all-clear ring of the old bell. Now hush."

Mr. Owl sounded the three calls once more, worried but defenseless. Eyeing Daisy – barely visible to him now – he drew closer, spreading his wing close around her and hoping she'd fall back to sleep. Meanwhile, he would continue to call for help and hope for the best.

■■

All the animals gathered around Sasha, large eyes worried and sad. Heathcliff and Mr. Mouse continued to try to revive the little bear, but there were no signs of movement. It was a very sad and very tensed moment.

Mr. Possum rubbed his eyes, trying not to be seen shedding tears. He crept closer to Sasha, touching his brown fur gently.

"Wake up Sasha," he said softly. "You're our hero, please wake up." He rubbed his eyes.

A caribou inched her way through the crowd until she was standing before Sasha. She eyed the little cub cautiously. Slowly, she lowered her head, smelling the bear. Her nose rubbed against Sashas', sniffing. Very gently and hesitantly she nudged into the ribs of the bear, as if giving a thorough examination, still smelling and probing the length of him. All the others watched without uttering a sound, hardly breathing. All eyes were upon the caribou and the little bear.

The caribou walked around to the other side of the cub, repeating the same procedure – continuing to sniff every part of the bear.

Minutes passed.

No one made a sound.

All were waiting to see if Sasha would waken or the caribou to speak. What seemed like hours passed before the silence was broken.

"Our little bear is very ill," the caribou sadly spoke.

"Wh ... wh ... what happened?" stammered Heathcliff. "He ... he was fine last night, and so proud of catching his fish."

The caribou nodded slowly, "I know. But he is ill and needs treatment, and fast. His heart is barely moving and his body temperature is dropping to a dangerous level. If he doesn't get help soon, he will die."

Mr. Mouse clung firmly to Sasha's neck.

"But he can't die! We must save him!" He kept pinching his friend's nose, wrapping his arms around the little bear's neck. "Wake up," he shrieked. "Sasha, wake up!"

The caribou gazed sadly at the others.

"Time is running out. Every second is vital to saving this little one."

All of the animals inched closer, "What can we do?"

"First we must make a warm bed for him. He is freezing cold, and if we don't get his body warmed up he'll die."

"Tell us what to do!" Heathcliff cried. "You are our healer; tell us and let's hurry!"

"All right," the caribou replied gently, "but I promise nothing. The little one is very ill."

The caribou looked at all the creatures, her friends for many years. She sadly took in their unhappiness and worries.

"First, we must gather some warm moss and pine boughs. Then we make a soft bed and lie him on it, covering him with rosemary and red clover. The red clover will break his fever, and if he has a bad infection inside his organs the clover will aid in flushing out all impurities."

"Bu-but ... Heathcliff stammered, "last night he was fine!"

"That was last night," the caribou firmly stated. "Mr. Possum, you stay here and watch over Sasha. Once we have him all covered with the moss and clover we'll water it down."

Everyone gasped.

"The sun will heat the moss and clover, causing steam to act as a steam flush-out. It will rid his body of the toxins. All you deer run and find some ginger root. Bring it back as soon as your hooves can carry you. Heathcliff, you stay with Mr. Possum and Mr. Mouse."

The deer ran as fast as they could go, in search of ginger root. Heathcliff, Mr. Possum, and the caribou all helped in lifting the little bear on the bed already arranged as the caribou told them to do. The little bear burned with fever, its golden brown fur soaking wet. They gently put him down on his soft bed and slowly started to cover him. Sasha let out a weak bellow, then fell back into his unconscious state.

Heathcliff's teeth chattered with fright. He wiped his eyes with his long ears, feeling sad at himself, that he was so hard on Sasha last night, about making up stories about his fishing skills. He just wanted Sasha to know they loved him, whether he was a great catcher of fish, or a hero, or not. They loved him for being who he was – a little cub without a family and all alone, before they all met and became such good friends. Why was it so important to the little bear to always be a hero? He should have said nothing, and not be so parental.

Mr. Mouse raced up next to Heathcliff, seeing his sadness.

"Heathcliff! Sasha is a great warrior! He will come out of this the victor like he bested old Rasputin!" He tapped his little foot, nervous himself but wanting to stay positive.

He yanked on Heathcliff's floppy ear, making them both laugh.

"That's better," Mr. Mouse grinned. "Come. Let's fill all our buckets with water from the stream by old Mr. Hare and pour it on the bed of moss and greens before the sun gets up."

They raced off, carrying a bucket in each paw towards the stream, hurrying to help get their friend well again.

The Practitioner

Now the duck wondered why her little friend hadn't been showing up at the stream, but when she heard the bell being rung throughout the forest she just knew something was wrong ... and no doubt the little cub was involved. Swimming up and down the stream, making sure she didn't wander too far from her nest, the duck frowned with worry. If only she could go further she'd find out what was happening. Maybe she could be of some help.

From time to time she would see old Rasputin stalking the flatlands on the far side of the stream, angry and being as arrogant as ever. Fluffing her brightly colored wings out, she swam quietly, deep in thought.

Maybe she could swim over to old Mr. Hare's place. Surely he would have heard something of all the ringing of the bell. She dove for food to feed her fledglings, coming up with moss and algae mostly. Her head and beak covered in debris, she ducked her head beneath the water to clean her face and beak off.

In such a short time of being with the cub, she had grown quite fond of him. She remembered the first time she had met his acquaintance: clumsy as all young-uns are, and trying to catch a fish.

She smiled, thinking how he would throw himself off the rock into the water, coming up empty handed ... but he never gave up trying to catch his fish.

First she would gather food for her family, then pay Mr. Hare a visit. He knew everything that happened in the forest, who was doing what – a regular busy-body, and not overly friendly ... but she would take over some carrots she spotted growing wild up stream a ways. That should bring a welcome from him.

Smiling, she dove beneath again, gathering enough food for the day, in case she was late getting back.

The hot sun broke through the lustrous pines, steam rising from the bed of moss and clover that covered the little bear, all except for his head. Everyone was busy gathering food for the day, in case he woke up early, in time for their midday meal. Berries were put to one side, the deer had returned with the ginger root, and dragging behind them – very carefully – was a hive filled with honey, the bees buzzing in and out of their hive, wondering what was going on.

Sasha slept on, making soft bellows as he tried to shake off the heavy bed of greens in his deep sleep. From time to time he would try to say something, then fall back into his feverish state.

The caribou looked on with frustration. She eyed all the creatures hovering around, sad and silent.

"Now, now." She scolded. "He will be all right. We just have to wait this out. I have done all I know to do in these situations. The hot sun will ease his pain if he has any, and rid his body of the toxins if he has eaten some bad food."

"But he only ate what we had here, and the fish caught last night," Heathcliff stammered.

"The fish," the caribou said hesitantly, "where did he catch it?"

Mr. Mouse edged towards Sasha looking concerned, gently reaching down to pat his ear. Looking up at the caribou, he shook he head. "We don't know. He would leave early every morning before any of us were awake, silently going to some stream to catch his fish."

The caribou looked confused.

"Why would he leave so early, and alone? After his experience with old Rasputin, wasn't he afraid to venture out alone?"

Mr. Possum came forward.

"Sasha wanted us to be surprised. He caught a lot of fish, but threw them all back, wanting the biggest one in the stream."

The caribou nodded. "The contests are coming up. It probably had something to do with that."

"Oh, it did!" exclaimed Mr. Mouse. "Sasha was planning on entering the fishing competition!"

"You'll make him well again, won't you?" the squirrels all asked in unison.

"We will all do what we can." The caribou gazed at all of them. "I have tended to most of you when you got hurt or ill. I will do all I can," she repeated.

"But he has to enter the contest!" Heathcliff cried. "I – I want ..."

"When is the day of skills held?" asked the caribou.

"Well, we had planned to have it four moons from now."

"Can't you change the time for later, when the little one recovers?"

"Yes! That's it!" Mr. Mouse cried. "We'll wait until Sasha gets well, then have it."

He looked around at all his friends. All the creatures, large and small, yelled with joy, "Yes! We'll wait until he's well!"

The day wore on with narry a change in the little bear. Heavy steam rolled up from the bed of clover and moss, sending a heavy fragrance throughout. Plans continued to be made, things to be done and preparations planned for the upcoming ball. Busy they all were, which helped pass the time.

There were guards posted to the North, to the South, to the East and West, watching and making sure old Rasputin wasn't seen even close to where they all were hiding out, their lairs and dens safely camouflaged with branches and greens. Now that one of theirs was ill, they had to take extra precautions.

Their healer stayed beside Sasha, grazing close by and nudging him softly throughout the day, letting him know he was not alone.

Rasputin on the Prowl

Rasputin slowly made his way to the top of the mountain, stopping from time to time, sniffing the air. Head held high, his mane soaked in sweat, he scanned the valley below him. The smell was coming from the direction of Old Sirus' place.

An evil grin appeared.

All at once he was hungry. He'd just have to risk getting shot at by the old buzzard, as he steadily made his way towards the chicken coup.

Plenty of hens there, and plump ones too, he licked his mouth hungrily.

He would have chicken for his noonday meal and check out what that strange smell was floating across the plains these past few days.

He perked his ears for any sound out of the ordinary. A red tail hawk screamed overhead, making its dive straight down at a high speed, talons spread wide as it grabbed up its kill, out looking for food of its own.

Rasputin arched his back, scowling at the intrusion.

He scanned the riverbed below him. He hadn't seen the cub for a while now. Had it been the mangy furball that he almost had for dinner that fateful night? He'd keep watch, and sooner or later he'd spot it again. He remembered on his hunts across the plains, spotting what looked like a small bear. Had his eyes been playing tricks on him again? He still couldn't figure out how he was fighting a bear cub one minute and the next a grizzly.

"Well, never mind," he growled. The next time he spotted the runt he would not get away. "So say your prayers, you mangy cur. You're living on borrowed time!"

He raised his large head, howling loudly, breaking the stillness around him.

He chuckled, "Run and hide you useless varmints! Rasputin is coming and one of you will die!" He made his way down, careful not to lose his footing. He had a chicken meal all planned and didn't want any setbacks.

Something ahead slithered across his path.

Old Rasputin stopped, backing slowly away. His eyes were intent on the rattlesnake in his path. The snake curled its body in a deadly attack pose, eyes beady and staring up at the wolf.

It made a quick strike, flinging its long neck out, hissing.

Rasputin stepped further back, circling the snake tentatively

... he would try to grab hold of its head. He hadn't had snake in

 a long time,

and didn't like

messing with

this one. He

always tried to

avoid them;

and besides, he

wasn't that

fond of vipers.

He much

preferred the

game of

running his

dinner down, their little hearts pumping with fear, trapping

them in a corner with no place to run – except right into his

mouth. He howled with glee, remembering all the morsels,

large and small, before they filled his empty stomach.

The rattler struck out again, missing Rasputin by only a few inches, as if mocking him, teasing him with skills of his own. Rasputin jumped back, letting a few yelps echo through the area.

Mad, he leaped towards the snake again, crouched half down, hind end circling in a death lunge as he made for the neck again. As fast as the speed of sound the snake reared up, tongue lashing as it struck out again, heavy foam frothing from the mouth. Its deadly eyes gave a venomous stare.

Wolf and snake glared at each other, intent on the kill.

Rasputin stared back, thinking of the strange smell that kept attacking his nostrils. Without losing eye contact he sniffed the air, not even moving his large sweaty head. There it was again, floating up in his nostrils, that same scent that he'd been smelling these last few days.

Backing slowly away from this cunning serpent, he pawed at the ground, not wanting his attacker to think he had won this battle. Safely at a distance he reared his head up, howling into the wind, satisfied he had the last word.

The rattler glared back, rattling his tail as if promising another time – another battle.

Rasputin growled one last look at the viper, then raced off down the mountain side, happy to be gone from that troublesome pest.

How he hated Rattlers! He was going for the chickens! Yes siree! – and less trouble!

Down he raced, mane flying behind him with the fury he felt within. He headed towards old Sirus' place, tongue hanging out in expectation of his meal ahead!

Old Sirus' place came into view, the old barnyard stretched out before him. He stopped short, sniffing the air. Somewhere that mean hayseed was wandering around feeding his livestock.

Rasputin slowly turned his head towards the chickens. The smell, known only to those inhabitants of a farm, was almost unbearable. The wolf twitched his nose, hoping to get the stench of manure out of his nostrils. Seeing his meal before him, he grinned – never had a meal so easy. He looked down at the chickens, all strutting towards the fence they were encased in, looking out towards where he crouched – safely hidden from view – in an old piece of brush left abandoned by the wind the day before.

Fluttering their wings, they made soft clucking sounds among themselves, sensing some thing or someone had intruded on their feeding time. Necks craning out to get a better look, they strutted along the outer edge, carefully surveying their territory.

"Get back away from the fence, you dumb hens, and eat your feed!" old Sirus shouted, picking up a stick to chase them away from the opening. "The fatter you are, the more of you varmints I can sell! Now git!"

Old Rasputin's ears perked up, a low growl deep in his throat. He stared at the skinny farmer, old and mean – almost as mean as he was. The chickens flew up out of the way of the stick, back towards their feed bin, forgetting all about what was outside their fence ... their safety zone.

"That's better! Now eat your fodder, while I mend some wire on the other end here! Something has tried to come through here and if my guess is right, it's not something but someone!

And my guess would be that mangy wolf I've seen around here lately."

He picked up his shotgun, muttering to himself as he walked angrily off towards the section of fence that needed repairing.

Old Rasputin stretched himself out, resting his large head on his paws, looking directly at all those tasty hens. "You mend your fences," he chuckled, "and while you're doing that, I'll have some nice juicy chickens for my midday meal!"

He'd just wait long enough until he was alone and could sneak up on those hens eating themselves into an exhausted state, then slowly creep up towards the opening he saw to the right of him and grab some tasty morsels.

"Couldn't be easier," he snickered.

Life was just too good!

Penelope's Visit to Crotchety Mr. Hare

The duck swam towards Mr. Hare's place, knowing he would have some news on Sasha. He always heard of what was going on, sometimes even before they happened it seemed. Nosiness and curiosity were his two outstanding qualities. He was crotchety, but way down deep inside was a good hare who looked after his family and wee ones, and his Mrs. in a loving but cautious way. He lived on old Sirus' farm and, seeing that old Sirus owned most of the land west of the river, settled far back against the bluff a long way from sight – perhaps three miles – choosing the bluff for protection against old Rasputin creeping along on all four sides of him and his family.

The duck paddled faster towards Mr. Hare's territory. The strange fragrance floated throughout the forest, the same smell she had been aware of for a few days now. What could it be? It wasn't a brush fire – she *knew* that smell, and so did everyone else!

Deep inside she was afraid it was connected to her friend, Sasha. She quickened her swim, wanting to get to the bottom of things. Maybe Mr. Hare could inform her of the strange smell that permeated throughout the forest lately. She knew he had a habit of stealing carrots and other vegetables from old Sirus, which could get him shot at if he wasn't careful. But on his nightly gathering of food for his family, maybe he heard something in those parts.

She hoped so.

On she swam. The shore came into view as she slowed her paddling, head turning from one side to the other in case the old farmer had her in his sights. He had "NO TRESSPASSING" signs posted on all sides of his property.

She gulped, feeling a lump in her throat from sheer nervousness. Her family depended on her for food and protection. Was she foolish in coming out here, in search of Sasha, whom she just met? Or at least in search of answers she had to have? She had good instincts, and this time she was driven to have answers to his whereabouts. She just felt that he was in dire trouble. She knew he liked her, had fun in their days fishing, and was happy. She was happy. Then it all ended. What had happened to him; he but a wee babe, trying to learn to fish and act like a bear. Saddened that he had lost his

ancestors and also their teachings of how to fish, and ways of

the bear for survival, she *had* to know if he was safe.

Her feet touched the bottom and she stepped out onto land,

fluffing out her beautiful, brightly colored feathers. Waddling up

onto the bank she headed directly towards Mr. Hare, hidden

among the carrot patch, filling his sack he had on his back full

of lettuce, carrots, and celery. Mr. Hare was so busy gathering

food for his family that he jumped with fear as the duck

approached, looking at him with reprimanding eyes.

"I could have been old Rasputin, about to have you for

dinner!" Nodding at his backpack filled with food, she added,

"From the looks, a hearty salad besides!"

"What do you want, you old busybody! And what are you

doing coming up on me like this?"

"I am here for some news. You can keep your sly comments

to yourself!" She eyed him steadily. "One day you will get

yourself shot, stealing from old Sirus! Then what would your

family do?"

"Never you mind!" Mr.Hare glared. "What is it you want?"

"Nothing that concerns you, so rest your fears. I am here to

see if there's any news on the bear cub, Sasha."

Mr. Hare leaned on his shovel, eyeing the nosy duck. "Aye, I have heard of some stories."

"Well?" the duck sighed. "Care to share with me what you've heard?"

"What's it worth to you, and why are you so interested?" The hare tugged on his ear, staring back at the impatient one before him.

"I am his friend! Care to tell me what you've heard?"

The hare chuckled, "If you be a friend, how is it you swim all this way to see if I – whom I have never met this cub –

should know of his whereabouts. It would seem, you being his friend and all, should know more of where he is than I."

The duck angrily fluffed her feathers out, waddling closer to the arrogant hare.

"I fear he is in trouble! We met a week ago, on the other side of the stream, a good half day's swim from here."

The hare eyed her cautiously, biting on a carrot.

Silence.

"I taught him how to fish! He wanted to enter the fishing event coming up soon, before the ball of the season. Won't you help me?" she asked impatiently.

"What else do you know of this Sasha?" Mr. Hare asked carefully.

"Only that he was almost eaten up by the mean Rasputin, and his little friend, Mr. Mouse, helped him escape, along with all his other friends ... Mr. Owl and–"

"Enough," the hare gruffly replied. "We can't be too careful. All I know is the little one's very ill. The smell that ripples throughout the land here is a healing potion, to try and save his life."

"What happened?" she asked, all agitated and nervous. "How do you know of this?"

"Isn't that why you paddled all this way?" Mr. Hare harshly answered. "Old Hare, the busybody; he knows of things happening around here that no one else does! Now you know! Now you can paddle on back and let me finish my gardening!"

"Do you know where he is?"

Seeing his impatience, she waddled closer, looking up at the disgruntled hare.

"Please ... tell me more."

"Women!" he muttered. "Word is, a few nights ago he became ill after eating a lot of fish! Some sort of celebration it was. Well anyway, the following morning he couldn't be wakened. This Mr. Mouse and Heathcliff sounded the alarm of the bells and the caribou was brought in."

The duck eyed him, not understanding.

Seeing her confusion, Mr. Hare cleared his throat.

"She's their practitioner. The smell that floats through these parts are some cockeyed beliefs that will make the unfortunate one well." He arched his eyebrow. "I for one don't believe in all that witchery."

"What do you believe in?" the duck stormed, eyeing him with impatience.

"Nothing!" Mr. Hare angrily retorted. "No one ever helped me! Why should I believe?"

"You should believe, because one day maybe you will need all this 'witchery' you call it. Maybe one day your family will be in dire need of help! That's why!"

She was furious, ruffling her feathers angrily.

"No one has ever wanted to help, and I don't see that changing!" He turned his back and started in on his picking of more vegetables for his family.

"You sure of that?" the duck persisted. "Everyone hereabouts knows you homestead on old Sirus's land. Everyone in these parts knows you steal his food and live off the fat of his land! No one had told the old goat! If he knew for sure, he would shoot you, and one more thing: Heathcliff brings you peat moss and berries! So there!"

She waddled back towards the water, indignant and anxious to be gone from this crotchety one.

"Wait!" Mr. Hare called.

She stopped, slowly turning around to gaze at him.

"Well, maybe they care some, but not that much! How do you know of such things?"

The duck smiled. "Perhaps I too am known as a busybody. Thank you for your news. I will try to find my friend."

She jumped off the bank, back into the water.

"Wait!" the hare repeated, and she swam back ... looking ... waiting. "He's out near the old quarry, half a day's swim to the west, hidden among the ponderosas. There's an old oak tree among the pines, towering high above. You can't miss the place." Seeing her smile, he added with a chuckle, "The steam follows most of the way. It shouldn't be that difficult, even for a duck."

She fluffed her wings again, eyeing him angrily. Seeing him chuckle, going back to his carrot picking, she smirked herself and happily swam back where she had come from. First she had to gather food for her own family, then try and find Sasha. Maybe she could be of some help.

Wolf in the House!

Rasputin edged closer to the chicken coup. Looking in the direction where old Sirus had wandered off, he crawled to the small opening at the end he had spotted. So the fox had been here; saves him the trouble and time digging his way in.

Crawling on his belly, he lay there, listening for the old buzzard with the shotgun. One thing he hated was buckshot. There was no sound but the hens pawing the ground in search of more food.

This was going to be just too easy; they were all too busy cackling among themselves to know that the mean, old wolf was about to have a tasty meal. He chuckled. Easing slowly through the torn chicken wire he started towards the hens, choosing the fattest one. He licked his mouth hungrily, taking another step forward.

Then it happened ... the worst nightmare of anyone inside a chicken house – being spotted by the hen in charge. She let out a scream of warning.

"WOLF IN THE HOUSE! WOLF IN THE HOUSE! run! Run! RUN! SOUND THE ALARM!"

Rasputin froze. He couldn't back out, as the barbed wire would get him. His only way out was to get all the way in, then back out as fast as his legs would carry him.

The chicken house was under attack! Every hen circled together in a tight group, ready to do battle and defend their territory. Screaming and sounding the alarm to their keeper, they glared back at the wolf, who was looking at the one he had chosen for his meal, fat and noisy as a field full of cannons firing off. He crawled inside the chicken coup then slowly stood on all fours, growling deep in his throat ... fangs bared ... ready for the attack. He took a menacing step towards the noisy hen, avoiding eye contact with the rest of the squawking misfits.

"WOLF IN THE HOUSE! WOLF IN THE HOUSE!" they yelled loudly.

Rasputin made a lunge at the fat hen just when a gunshot was fired. He spun around, eyes filled with instinct to kill, feathers hanging from his snarling mouth. Another shot rang out – barely missing him.

He raced to the opening, not wanting to waste one second. The fat hen was standing angrily in front of the hole he had crawled through, still screaming, "WOLF IN THE HOUSE!"

Rasputin took another lunge at the loudmouth, only to feel the nick of a bullet go flying by. He let out a yelp that woke the forest. Another followed as he made a fast run towards the back of the coup and jumped over the fence, missing another bullet by a thread. He circled the hens, promising the bunch of squealing hyenas that he would be back!

"Another time! Another meal!"

Body stretched out as far as it would go, he raced as fast as he could, dodging bullets that came far too close to his head. Swerving left and right, he put as much space between the nasty hayseed holding the rifle and himself that he could. Some buckshot splattered against his hind end, causing another yelp.

Finally out of danger, he stopped behind some brush to seek cover while he caught his second breath. Shaking out his sweaty coat, he examined himself carefully, yelping from time to time in the process.

"BUCKSHOT!"

He hated the stuff. It could really hurt and lodge in the fur, tearing the skin beneath. Licking his wounds and cleaning them the best he could, he sauntered into the stream, washing all the remains of the powder away.

Dusk was upon him. He swam around some to rid the stench off him of hens and bad memories. Paddling slowly, he rested his head on the water, lazily getting back his breath. He wondered how the fox had made out, or whatever had made the hole in the fence. There were a lot of hens there. Next time he would get one or two.

Making his way out of the water, he shook himself dry and started his run again. It was time to eat, and he'd settle for a couple hares this night. Tomorrow was another day. Raising his head, he let out a piercing howl. Rasputin was hungry, mad, and about to fill his stomach!

A small calf wandered around here somewhere. He knew the smell. Grinning, he raced on. It didn't much matter with him. Hare, calf, or even a bear cub sounded yummy. He felt better already. Life was just too good, yes siree! He'd settle with the old hayseed soon, that was a promise! No one took a shot at him and lived to tell about it! He'd kill all his hens, then come after him.

The heavy fragrance drifted to his nostrils again. He slowed to a stop, sniffing around. He hadn't smelled it downstream where the hens were. Whatever it was had to be in this area. After he claimed his kill, he'd check it out again.

Sasha's Past

The duck swam on, eager to locate Sasha. Her family was safely covered, her nest safely hidden from predators, and well fed. On the way back from Mr. Hare she gathered up a lot of food, in case she stayed away longer from her nest than expected.

She had to find Sasha.

She paddled faster, hoping to locate the tall oak tree that hovered over the plains. She smiled, thinking of Mr. Hare. Cantankerous, but deep down – if you were willing to dig deep enough – there was a nice hare. She wondered why he didn't like to show that good side. Everyone made up stories of him and would tell their young ones of old Mr. Hare.

Off in the distance behind her, she heard Rasputin's angry howl.

She shivered, picking up speed. Darkness was settling in. She was glad she asked her friend to sit with her family. If she was late arriving back to the nest, at least her family had a sitter.

Chores all completed, food gathered and meal eaten, Heathcliff and all the friends of Sasha silently sat around in a circle, watching the caribou change the blankets of heated pine and herbs. The sun had gone down a couple of hours ago, but steam still rose up from where their friend lie, still and hardly breathing. From time to time he would toss about like he was needing to get up or say something; then almost as fast as he moved and tossed, would find solace in his deep sleep.

Heathcliff nudged Mr. Mouse, who sat beside him deep in thought.

"Mr. Mouse, do you think Sasha's ancestors will visit him again?"

Mr. Mouse looked towards the sky, the moon slowly breaking through the clouds, sending eerie shadows where the little bear lie.

"I hope so," the little mouse sadly answered.

Mr. Possum and all the rest of their friends quietly discussed their plans for the coming contest, each deciding on the skills they would each show off. It was a solemn time, but each night they worked on their plans for the big festivities coming up. They had decided to wait until Sasha fully recovered before holding the competition. Meanwhile, the ladies sewed, making garlands for the coming ball and fancy gowns for their young ones, in search of their mates.

They all kept busy, praying to the Great Spirit to make their friend well again. How they missed Sasha ... his tall tales and vivid stories he had to tell. He was just a very funny little bear:

clumsy, and tripping over his large paws sometimes – that were growing faster than he was – but that was all right. He would joke and say one morning he would awaken to his body as large as his paws!

He would mend. He *had* to.

Heathcliff nudged his friend again.

Mr. Mouse looked at Heathcliff, wondering what bothered him.

"Don't you think it strange that heat still comes out from the blanket of herbs and pines? The sun went down hours ago."

....

Sasha raced ahead of his ancestors on their outing in the forest where the stream flowed freely, their favorite picnic area.

"He will grow to be a fine grizzly," the dad said, watching their son chase after a butterfly.

Seeing the stream up ahead, the little bear raced to it; stumbling, and falling to the ground – he didn't care. Life was one big adventure. Rolling around on the ground, he looked back at his ancestors, happy they were close by. He bellowed back at his ancestors, happy they were close by. He bellowed loudly doing summersaults, trying to touch his paws; then he jumped, trying to walk on hind legs only, like he would see them do. Down he fell again, and rolling over on his back; small and round as a butterball, he gazed at his ancestors.

"I am going fishing! I am going to catch the largest fish in the stream!"

Off he ran to the water's edge, throwing himself into the raging river, belly first!

His ancestors watched with amusement, love etched into

their large brown faces, eyes filled with pride ... the father saying, "We will teach him to fish soon. He's almost ready. In the meantime, let him play."

The mother smiled in agreement, "Yes, he's still too young. At least he loves the water, that's a plus."

They would give their son the freedom of play and check out all the wonders of the earth. They were always close by.

Sasha jumped back on the large rock, slipping back into the water a few times before he stood looking back at shore where his family stood, proud and happy.

"Be careful son."

"Dad! I see a BIIIGGG fish! I am going to catch him for our dinner!" be bellowed, plunging belly-first back into the water.

A loud shot rang out ... then another.

Sasha became an orphan this day, hiding out in the water behind the large rock he dove from ... which saved his life.

■■■

Heavy steam rose from Sasha's bed of pines. Sasha made soft bellowing sounds. Heathcliff and Mr. Mouse walked over to where their friend lie, wishing they could talk to him. The caribou kept nudging the bear, as if rocking him. Back and forth she nuzzled him, speaking in a soft, reassuring voice known only between forest creatures. She looked at the hare and mouse.

"He will mend. He has to do this on his own. We can only do so much; the rest is up to the little bear, and his will to live."

"B-but," Heathcliff stammered. "He has friends now. He's no-not alone anymore."

"I know," answered the caribou.

"Why doesn't he wake up?" asked the mouse. "Is he going to die?"

He looked down where Sasha lie, all covered with the sweet smelling blanket of moss and pines.

"Your little friend is going through some traumatic events while he lies sleeping. I don't know what they are, but he does; and once he comes to terms with what happened to him, he will recover. That is ... if he wants to."

"Do you think it's the bad experience he had with Rasputin in the well," asked Mr. Possum, who quietly joined them.

"I wouldn't think so," answered the caribou. "He was happy telling all his stories about that night, and how he found all his new friends. No. There has to be something more traumatic.

He's having a hard time accepting something in the past that happened. There seems to be a lot of sadness and pain. He bellows softly these last few days and nights. Your little bear is in serious trouble unless he can get through this."

The caribou eyed each of them.

"What do you know of this one?"

"I ran into him while out fetching some food for Heathcliff and myself, after winning the race," Mr. Mouse said. "I ran smack in front of him and we both went toppling down the hill, falling into the old abandoned well to the east of us."

Heathcliff rubbed his long floppy ear and Mr. Possum wrapped his long tail around himself, wondering what had happened to his little friend.

The caribou continued the rocking.

"I know!" yelled Mr. Mouse. "He ate too much fish!"

"No. It's much more than that. When Sasha wakens, only he can tell us. Meanwhile, we all must continue to get the rosemary and moss to keep the herb working. It will help. The rest is up to the little bear."

Penelope's Search for Sasha

The duck was almost there. She could see the tall oak hovering among the ponderosas. All she had to do was follow the fragrance that steamed through the forest. It was dark now, and she was thankful for the full moon that shone bright throughout the night.

Out in the distance, she heard the sound of a lone wolf.

It was the howl of old Rasputin, she was almost certain. There was an angry sound to his howls, angry and menacing. She hoped he was far away and would keep going.

Shifting her gaze back to the steam coming from the trees, she turned and paddled towards shore. Sasha had to be here close by. Old Hare had mentioned that he was ill, and the practitioner was tending to him with steaming herbs and peat moss.

Once more this day her feet touched bottom. She stepped out of the river and jumped up on the bank, fluffing her feathers. She looked around.

All was quiet.

Almost too quiet, she thought.

Another piercing howl sounded into the night, this time closer. The duck hurried into the forest, seeking cover. Nervous, but determined to find her new friend and see if he needed help, she waddled on, hoping she could outsmart and outrun old Rasputin – if she had to. That was impossible, but it gave her a cheery thought as she entered the deep forest.

She stopped, trying to get a sense of direction for returning back to the river. Looking around, she scanned the area she was in. Tall ponderosas stood overhead, and then she spotted the large statuesque oak standing proudly among the pines.

That's the area! She thought happily. *I am not far from where little Sasha is.*

Deep fragrances wafted towards her and she waddled on where she barely made out the path of steam breaking through the density of trees. Thankful she had the full moon, but at the same time a little afraid of being seen by that predator, Rasputin, she bravely made herself follow the stream of fragrances. She smelled the herb rosemary. Now she knew *that* smell. Rosemary was a cure-all; a good antioxidant to mend most any illness. Trudging on, she hoped it worked on her friend.

The sound of twigs breaking through the silence gave her a start. It was behind her.

She picked up speed, going as quietly as possible for a duck with large webbed feet, walking through the forest so late at night.

The sound came again.

She ran, flew a few paces, then ran and flew some more, careful not to fly into a tree. She hid behind a moss covered rock three times her size. She waited – no sound. Was her mind playing tricks on her?

Probably so, she told herself. She was not liking this idea of trekking through strange places, alone and not knowing how far she'd have to go from the river before finding Sasha.

On her journey once more she drew closer to the stream. Then, as if by some great magic, she came into a small opening surrounded by trees and the oak towering high above. Soft murmurings were heard and she headed towards the sounds, quiet but still audible. She looked around, making out a caribou beside the stream that seeped through the land. Smiling, she knew it had to be their practitioner.

Looking carefully around the little enclosure, protected by all the camouflage of brush and alarms hung from trees, she stared at the small clump of animals ... some asleep, and some talking in low sounds. There were skunks, a family of possums, squirrels, and all creatures large and small, nestling close together. Turning to where the murmurings were coming from, she spotted a mouse and hare. Her gaze shifted back to the caribou, gently nudging a bed of peat moss and where the steam was drifting from.

Heathcliff and Mr. Mouse quickly looked up, sensing they had a stranger in their area. The cry of Mr. Owl high up in the tree gave a reassuring answer to their fears. It was a duck, coming to help in any way possible.

Heathcliff and Mr. Mouse slowly rose and walked quietly towards the duck, careful not to wake the others. Heathcliff was the first to offer welcome:

"You gave us a start. I am Heathcliff, and this is my friend, Mr. Mouse. We have a friend that's very ill."

"I know," the duck answered. "My name is Penelope. I am a friend of your little bear, Sasha. I heard he was very ill."

"But ... but ..." gibbered Mr. Mouse.

"Let me explain," the duck softly replied. "I met Sasha five

moons ago early one morning, before the sun came up. I will tell you the story, if I may first see him. I have traveled a long way, and not far from here I heard sounds in the forest behind me. I think maybe Rasputin followed me. It pains me to say this, but I think I led him to your retreat here. I am sorry."

Mr. Mouse raced to wake everyone and to stand guard, to sound the alarm if Rasputin was sighted. Mr. Owl watched, hearing enough, and took off to a tree closer into the density of trees surrounding the enclosure where Sasha and all the animals were.

Heathcliff led Penelope towards the bed of steam. "Our practitioner is tending him with herbal remedies and steam. She says it will bring the poisons out; and once this is done, maybe Sasha will live."

Heathcliff gulped sadly, looking at Sasha.

The caribou looked up, eyeing the exhausted looking duck. "Are you a friend of this one?"

"Yes," the duck replied. "We met while he was catching fish." She spoke with a purpose. She didn't want them to know or ever find out that their friend didn't know how to fish. It was so important to Sasha that they thought him a great catcher of fish. Penelope swallowed hard, looking down at the sweaty little bear, moaning softly in a deep sleep.

"Where was he fishing?" asked the concerned caribou.

"The river west of here runs towards old Sirus' place. My nest is a half day from his farm. I was out skimming the water looking for food for my fledglings when I spotted the little bear." Seeing the confused look on the caribou, Penelope added, "The river is clean. I catch food there all the time."

Mr. Mouse raced back to take part in the conversation. "Do you think he got hold of a poison fish?"

"He caught a very large one; then, wanting to get right back to where his friends were, I told him to go. We were going fishing the next morning at my place. When he didn't show up for a few days I was concerned something had happened to him."

"How did you find us?" Mr. Possum asked, joining the small group.

"This is Mr. Possum," the caribou introduced.

The duck greeted him, then went on with her story.

"I swam down to Mr. Hare's place. He knows everything that happens around these parts. Not the friendliest of hares, but after awhile I convinced him I was Sasha's friend. Well anyway, he told me how to get to the area where all the steam was coming from."

Penelope stared at the steam.

"How come there is steam when the sun went down many hours ago?"

Heathcliff and Mr. Mouse nudged each other, having asked the same question the night before.

"It's a mystery," the caribou agreed, "but a mystery that works good for the little one."

"I think he ate too much fish!" Mr. Mouse exclaimed in a hushed tone. "Would that make him sick?"

Saddened eyes looked for answers, gazing at their healer, then the duck.

"No," the caribou firmly replied. "It is something much worse than overeating."

Penelope waddled quietly over to Sasha, who was still bellowing in painful cries. She lowered her long graceful neck, talking quietly into his ear.

"Sasha, it's me ... your friend the duck. Remember, we fished together?"

Sasha swayed from side to side, restless and agitated. The duck stepped back, tears in her eyes.

"If it isn't the fish that he ate the night before, what could it be? What did you and Sasha talk about those days? Maybe there's a clue that we missed," the caribou stated. "He had been feeling well, went off to catch fish, raced back to his friends all happy and healthy, staying up half the night laughing and trading tales. He dreamed of entering the skill competitions and said he wanted to enter the fishing event. That morning, shortly after, Mr. Mouse woke us, saying Sasha wouldn't wake up. He was burning with fever and his fur soaking wet. Others shared the fish ... so it wasn't that. If it was a poisoned fish, others would be ill. No. We are missing something. Let's start at the beginning."

The caribou looked at Penelope.

"Tell us everything you know about Sasha."

The duck looked apprehensive.

"If you want to save his life, you must. Maybe it will help find what started his sickness."

Penelope thought fast, every event running through her

mind. One thing she would leave out was Sasha not knowing

how to fish.

A Visit from Sasha's Ancestors

The duck began again:

"I was out skimming the river for food and enjoying the solitude of the early morning when I spotted the little bear fishing. It was fascinating to watch. He spotted me and swam over to where I was, and we struck up a friendship. We spent the rest of the day fishing and enjoying each other's companionship."

"Did he speak of anything that perhaps had been bothering him?" Heathcliff asked.

"No. He told me of his friends he had met and that they were his family now."

They all looked at Penelope.

"Friends ... meaning all of you here."

"Did he mention anything about his ancestors?" Mr. Mouse asked quickly.

Penelope thought for a while, all of the others waiting for her reply.

"Let me think," she slowly answered. "He did say that his ancestors were dead ... shot by poachers, I remember him saying."

"Hmmm," the caribou said. "Where was he when they were killed?"

"I don't know," slowly replied Penelope.

"What are you thinking?" Heathcliff asked their healer.

"It may not be important, but if Sasha witnessed his ancestors' killing, it could be the reason he became so ill."

"But how?" asked Mr. Mouse.

"Sasha had been fishing. Maybe it brought back painful memories he blocked out. Now if Sasha

saw his family killed, and stayed hidden for awhile until the poachers left, then for a young bear to see all this – or *any* of us – wouldn't that be a traumatic experience? Maybe one that

would leave such scars that sleep would be the only answer –
to forget."

"But he was happy. He liked being with us," Mr. Possum
exclaimed.

"I know. But the mind is a fickle one. If the pain becomes too
much to handle – cases such as this – one goes into a deep
sleep, reliving that fateful day as if it happened all over again. In
cases like this, the one who suffers from such a memory oft
times never wakes up. To wake up means to come to terms
with their loss. Sometimes they're not capable of doing this."

The caribou looked around at all of Sasha's friends.

"I'm not saying this is what's happening; and I'm not saying
this is what will happen, if it is the reason for his
unconsciousness. We have to wait. Maybe the Great Spirit will
mend your little friend. There is nothing else I know to do. We
must keep the guards posted. Right now we are vulnerable for
any attack. The steam floats among the forest, we have lost
much sleep, and our strengths are very low. We will be easy
pickings for predators ... especially Rasputin, who swore
revenge on the bear and each of you."

I want all of you to eat and take turns standing guard. When your post is over, sleep. There're enough of us to keep our retreat here safe. Meanwhile, keep up your chores and planning for the upcoming festivities. It will take your minds off your friend and bring some positive thoughts to us all ..." the caribou looked at Sasha, "for him too.

In the meantime, we'll continue our herbal treatment. If nothing else, it's soothing and will break his fever."

■■■

Rasputin stalked the forest, heading towards the area where all the steam was coming from. His eyes were in menacing slits as he swore with each step he took that this night he would destroy them all ... starting with the little furball.

A low growl resounded deep within. This night he would have so much to eat; he'd have to chase everything he saw move, for the next week, just for the exercise and to lose the weight he put on by his hearty feast this night.

He howled with glee, his belly empty but knowing that soon he would be so full he would have a nice long after-meal sleep. Rasputin would win this night, oh yes siree!

■■■

"Sasha, you have slept far too long. It's time to wake up."

Sasha looked through the heavy mist, trying to see his ancestors. His mother and father gazed at him with sternness.

"Wake up son."

"But I can't!" Sasha cried.

"Yes you can. All you have to do is open your eyes."

"But ... I can't!" the little bear repeated.

"You must have the will to do so," his mother spoke.

Sasha swayed from one side to the other, weary and sad. "I saw the men with big guns. I hid behind the large rock I was fishing from. I should have fought them and tried to save my family."

"Sasha!" his father rebuked. *"You couldn't have saved us. They crept up on your mother and myself without notice or warning. We were gone before you entered the water. You were lucky they didn't see you."*

"But I need you! I need you to teach me the ways of the bear!" Sasha cried.

"No you don't. Your duck friend taught you to fish," his

father smiled. *"You caught a big fish, son,"* he chuckled, *"and I was very proud of you."*

"You saw?"

"We see everything you do," his mother smiled, *"even you telling all your stories! Threw all the small ones back, well I never!"*

"Now now," his father admonished. "You used to enjoy my tall tales. Our son takes after me in that area. He is a natural-born storyteller. You bring a lot of joy to your friends, listening to your tales; but you must find your own strengths, my son. We can only do so much."

Sasha opened his eyes wide, walking over to his father.

"But how do I find my own strengths when I don't know what they are?"

"It won't be hard to do, my son. It is the nature of life, to tap into areas that are a natural way of life to each creature put onto this earth. You are a bear. The ways of the bear will come to you each day of your life. Each day you will be shown things you can't begin to understand, but it will get easier as you meet each new day."

"I don't understand," the little bear said. "How will I know if I don't understand?"

"You will, my boy." His mother reached down and patted his head. "This natural phenomenon is called 'instinct.' All creatures in the life force have it. It teaches even unborn ones while in the belly of the womb. It comes from the family one has yet to meet. It's a natural miracle, just like your surviving.

If you hadn't jumped into the water at exactly the same time we were taken from you, you too would have been killed."

"I wish ..."

"No! Sasha, never wish for death! Your life is just beginning. You already have a lot of friends. And now you met a duck who taught you how to fish like bears do ... and not like an otter," his father chuckled.

Sasha loved his head being rubbed. He leaned into his mother, all warm and loving.

"Will we ever play together again?" He looked up into his mother's deep brown eyes, filled with love and sadness.

"Yes, son, one day we will, and we'll be a family again. But until the Great Spirit is ready for this to happen you must get well and cherish each day of your life here on this earth, and learn all the ways of the bear."

"One day son, you'll grow into a fine grizzly and find a mate to start a family of your own ... but first you must wake up. We watch your friends tending you. We had a word with the one who is called a practitioner. We had a difficult time communicating, as it's a hard task to do unless we get through our loved ones. Tis the way it is. We will help in some ways my

boy, but we can't do your work for you. You have to gather up strength where you have it and fight this thing you're going through."

Hesitating, he gazed down at his son.

"Remember who you are," his father smiled.

"Who am I?" the little bear asked.

"You are Sasha, the great warrior!"

Sasha bellowed loudly, grinning from ear to ear. "I am Sasha! I am a great WARRIOR!"

"That's our boy ..."

Sasha saw them slowly fade out of sight.

"No! Don't go!" he cried.

They sadly looked at their little cub.

"We are always with you, son. Never are we far away from you. Find your inner strengths. Every star high above are the spirits of lost loved ones. When you become sad or lonely, look to the heavens. We will be watching over you. You'll be able to see us from time to time in your difficult times. You will know we are looking down on you with strength to carry you through. Goodbye, son ... remember who you are."

Rasputin's Retribution

Rasputin stopped dead in his tracks, hind legs planted firmly into the ground – ready for attack. He perked his ears and listened. There was indeed something going on in these parts lately, and he would find out exactly what it was! Sounds he heard ... he remembered the same sounds coming down into the well that horrible night not that long ago. He recalled how the little runt he had trapped there kept talking to himself. The same sounds were heard this night.

He raised his large head, heavy mane wet and covered with moss and twigs from running through heavy brush and swimming across the river.

"I'll find you, you mangy cur. Tonight I will eat you up before you can say 'hippity-hop!'"

He laughed at his own joke, remembering that flea-ridden mouse shouting endearments to the lopsided hare. Those same voices troubled him. Was the furball so demented that he always spoke in different voices? Different tongues?

He chuckled. He thought he had heard that expression outside a run-down church, everyone gathering for a picnic social or spiritual uplifting. He had helped himself to all the food in dainty baskets and even gulped down some of their "dandelion wine," he thought he heard them call it. Well, no matter. He feasted and drank. Snickering, he was glad old Sirus wasn't there with his buckshot. He was so wobbly he could hardly make it back in the forest before being seen.

He'd leave that stuff alone from now on.

His nips from here on would be the behinds of his next meal.

His thoughts once more centered on the mangy cub. If he was *that* crazy to always talk to himself, and so different answering himself, did he have rabies? He sure didn't want rabid food!

He scowled. If he chased it down and scared it enough, maybe the demented bear would drop dead from fear and exhaustion! No threat there to himself, and purpose of revenge served! He liked that.

Howling with distorted snarls, he made his way deeper into the thicket, enjoying the game of cat and mouse. He laughed. His jokes were so good maybe he should join one of those circus caravans he had seen roll through here sometimes. They served great food ... especially the kind he helped himself to.

A low, contented sound came from deep inside. The snapping of dead twigs brought him back to the present. There were too many noises going on ... he'd have to stop daydreaming. He heard the sound again and old Rasputin's eyes glared into the brush ahead. Something was in there.

Was it a rattler? He *hated* snakes; never knew for certain what they would do or when. Cunning and quick, they always posed a threat to him. Did he want to check it out, or just

continue his journey towards the steam and smell floating out at him? He knew deep inside it would lead him to the furball. How he knew, he didn't have the foggiest. He just knew, and his sixth sense told him to continue.

He eyed the brush, seeing it move as something was scrounging around looking for food. He grinned evilly. Maybe he would have a small appetizer before meeting up with the runt. Besides, he wasn't too sure anymore if he wanted to risk eating tainted food.

Old Rasputin needed some substance in his belly – not much noise, so small prey this was. At least he wouldn't have to work too hard gulping this one down.

He snickered, "I done talked myself into an early repast."

He crouched low, stealthily stalking towards the movement in front of him.

"Piece of cake," he chuckled. "Come out, come out, whoever you are," he chanted, enjoying the chase before the kill.

Pawing at the ground to sound the alarm, he waited for his meal to make a run for cover. It were times like these he dreamed of ... chasing the surprised little weaklings before he ate them up!

He waited ... ready to pounce ... feet spread ... waiting to begin his triumphant chase.

He scowled.

No sound.

No movement.

Well, he would just have to aid the frightened little coward.

He stuck his nose to the ground, sniffing to pick up scent. He hadn't all night to flush it out, he was on a mission! He peered inside the thicket, cautiously and ready to attack – body arched, teeth bared.

Quietness set in. He dug the ground again, easing slowly through the opening he caught sight of. His large furry head looked around, trying to make out a form. He could smell a familiar scent that he knew was not a stranger to him. He quietly sniffed again, picking up that same smell he was sure he had been around before.

He growled ... still no sound or movement. Following his senses he lunged ahead, growling as he scanned the darkness.

"HA!"

In the back, hiding beneath a piece of fallen tree, was the

little coward. He cursed, feeling the sting of a cactus. Mad and

impatient, he

sprang on top of

the piece of

vermin, taking

hold of it in his

mouth and

backing out as

careful as he

could to try to

avoid getting

pricked again. Whatever it was he caught, it was a wiry thing,

its heart beating as fast as a streak of lightning. He could feel

the death-fear he knew so well of all his victims ... part of the

joy of his hunts.

Easing himself out into the clearing, he held on to his prize

firmly as he walked over to the clearing to enjoy his tasty meal.

He dropped it between his paws, hoping it would run and he

could chase it down the right way before his kill. He sniffed the head, smelling that scent again. He looked close, studying his kill. What was it that made him so intimate with the smell? With his huge paw he flipped his kill over. It had to be dead, otherwise it would have run for safety.

"You mangy little coward! You took all the fun out of my

hunt!" Rasputin growled, not sure if he wanted to eat dead meat.

The moon broke beneath the clouds as Rasputin stared down at his prize, knocking it back over where he had inspected the back. He pawed at the sides, knocking it over again ... he was studying the face of a black wolf pup.

He moaned into the night, raising his furry head to howl with a cry never heard from old Rasputin before this night. It was a cry of loneliness and forgotten ties of his family pack. Full of heartache, he continued to howl way into the night; then pawing at the little pup, he nuzzled its head – Rasputin's eyes glazed over with wetness.

He bent down, licking the little pup's face, washing away the dirt that covered the little one's face, who was trying to hide from the mean old wolf. He lied down beside the pup, cradling it between his large paws, his head bent to nuzzle it gently.

All else was forgotten: all the thoughts of revenge and killing the bear cub and making a quick kill of all the friends of the wee cub. Rasputin had only one thought; one passion; one journey.

Wails of despair and regret shattered the still night. He refused to let go of the pup, black as the night around him and as small as the rock he had hidden behind, in fear of being eaten up. Rasputin remembered a long time ago when he was held this way, nestled into warmth and so much love; he recalled that time so detailed that he almost felt the heartbeat of his mother.

Rasputin gulped, swallowing hard as though his throat was nothing but the pinpoint of a pine needle, like those scattered around him. He rested his heavy jaw against the unmoving pup. He inhaled with sadness once more, smelling that sweet smell of pines and peat moss in the distance.

He continued washing the face of the little black pup, furry and fat as a butterball. Making low sounds in his throat, as if singing a lullaby, he hugged deeper into the soft fur, smelling the wolf scent even at such a tender age. His thoughts were scattered, going way back in time when he was but a wee babe; soft, gentle growls were remembered, the warmth of his mother holding him as close as he was holding this one.

Snuggling closer into the damp fur, moist from fear of being attacked, the little one was still, all his worries over at such a tender age. Old Rasputin moaned with sadness and regret. Cupping the pup tighter to his warmth, he wondered how this one came to be alone and still a babe. He remembered the story of poachers being seen in these woods. Had they shot his mother and father and left this one to die all alone, helpless and hungry?

He twitched. Hunger! If he hadn't frightened his own into an early grave he would have starved anyway. These thoughts didn't bring Rasputin any release from scaring the wits out of a pup of his own kind. He shook with remorse and disgrace. What had happened to him throughout the years?

Eyes glazed with water, he thought back to the night so many years ago – years blocked from memory – memories too painful to face.

Remembering, he howled painfully hour after hour throughout the night, paws wrapped tightly around the black pup, comforted in his sadness that he wasn't alone.

Rasputin's Story

A long time ago, a little wolf pup was born. His ancestors named him, Rasputin. Oh how they waited and waited to bear a son. His ancestors were growing older and had not yet conceived. Wolves mate for life. They met many years before out running with the pack. They hunted. They shared their food and ran throughout the nights, full of dreams and hopes of their future.

There were thirty of them running with the pack. They played, hunted, shared meals and birthed their young; they made plans for all their families, as they all *were* family. Two wolves eyed each other one night, after being members of the same pack for years. It just happened. Over the remains of chewing on a carcass, their eyes met and a low growl of acceptance was heard between the two wolves sizing the other one up.

Slowly, one eased his way closer to the female, bringing food as a gift, dropping it at her front paws. Growling deeply, she looked at the handsome wolf, bringing his offering of courtship. She nudged into him, sides touching, and she bit off pieces of the carcass. Dropping at his front paws, she shared the food brought as a token of mating. Sly glances were shared among the others in the pack, growls of happiness and encouragement to the two new mates.

Time passed ... many years of planning and trying to birth a son. The older they became, the more need to have a son to carry their name. Just when all seemed lost to bring forth a pup – it happened, a miracle actually. At a very late age the female became fertile, bringing a beautiful wolf pup into being. They were finally fruitful and all their dreams throughout the years had been made possible.

Celebrations among the pack were plentiful. The little pup was one of the most beautiful they had ever seen, and so playful and smart ... way beyond his years. He was loved. He was watched over day and night as they were all worried about men with large rifles killing them off for no reason at all ... just for the sport of it – the kill – the trophies hung up on walls, displaying their vanity and false heroism.

On day, Rasputin's mother and father left their beautiful little pup with the elder of the pack, so they could run with the others, trying to locate the men with large guns to drive them

out of the territory. They never returned. They were all shot down like sitting ducks.

Rasputin wandered alone with the elder for three years, trying to survive from hunger and getting shot. Then, at a tender age, Rasputin woke up with the elder's paws wrapped tightly around him, as if shielding him from harm. His only protector was dead ... he died from stress and old age. From

that day on, little Rasputin, still only a young wolf not old enough to have his own say in a pack – and too young to be accepted – ran wild on his own until he talked himself into running with the pack that later kicked him out, when he became too powerful, thinking on his own.

He was lonely. He was brokenhearted at losing his mother and father at such a tender age. He had just started to know what warmth and love was, when they were killed. He turned to hate and sadness, seeking revenge on every living thing that tried to get too close. He became the loner – the angry one of the pack, snarling and wanting to strike back. He was warned never to return to the pack unless he wanted to be killed. Bad memories always resurfacing, he felt betrayed by his own, and always left out and alone.

Throughout the years he became hard, cruel, and played savage games of pursuit in making his kills. He lost touch with who he was, or where he came from. He had no one to care for, or anyone to care for him. He only was known as the mean old Rasputin! An outcast.

He sighed heavily, picking the pup up in his mouth and making his way towards the smell he had been following. Weary, in need of food and sleep, he trekked on, content to have someone close to him on his journey.

So tired from exhaustion, he stumbled, almost falling to the ground. He stopped and found himself next to the river's edge. Thirsty, he gently eased the pup to the ground, drinking heavily of the river while keeping his bloodshot eyes on the little one. Quenching his thirst, he opened his mouth and spewed water on the still pup.

Slowly ... very slowly ... the little one opened its bright yellow eyes, gazing intently at the large wolf before him.

Rasputin blinked.

He hesitantly lowered his head, sniffing the small face in front of him. Had his senses left him too? Was there still life in the pup he carried around half the night? A low growl escaped his throat. He nudged the still pup.

No movement.

Rasputin rested his paw on top of the little one's head, staring into his frightened eyes, not daring to blink. Another low growl he gave; he nipped his ear.

The little pup let out a helpless yelp.

Rasputin nudged him some more, pawing into the ground, hind end in the air as he circled his captive, gently sniffing his

head. Yellow eyes met the other, sizing each other up. The little
pup tried to break free from the huge paws holding him down.
Rasputin saw fear in the little pup's face.

Slowly, Rasputin took his paws away, gazing down intently,
watching closely as the wolf pup slowly stood, wobbling from
side to side as he took one very careful step away from the
giant wolf hovering in front of him. He let a growl escape his
throat ... one last effort to defend himself. Facing Rasputin, the

pup slowly
backed up,
uttering
growls and
pawing at the
ground as if
challenging
the big one to
fight.

Rasputin
watched in
fascination, seeing himself at a tender age. He gently growled
back, backing away from the little one, but careful not to be too

far away. The little pup raised his head, calling into the night, faint but doing what he knew wolves were supposed to do, remembering his ancestors telling him stories of the wolf.

Rasputin was frozen in time. He gave the little survivor all the time he needed, watching his every movement, slow and weak. Still eyeing each other, not daring to blink, Rasputin watched the pained and sad face of the pup. He gently growled back, sniffing his scent.

A low growl tremored in response as the pup tried to escape. One step – then down in a heap the little one fell.

Rasputin stepped carefully forward. He nudged the pup's leg very carefully, not wanting to cause him any more alarm or pain than he had already. He nipped onto his ear again – no sound. He bit a little more firmly – no response.

He howled into the night, his cries ringing throughout the air. Picking up the pup by the neck, he trotted towards the fragrance, never knowing such sadness and loneliness before ... not since his youth.

A Cry for Help

Heathcliff jumped, nose twitching nervously, coming wide awake. He looked around, seeing only the caribou tending to the herb bath. His little eyes shifted all around their retreat, safely from old Rasputin, until Sasha mended. All was still. Had he had a bad dream? He looked over at Mr. Mouse, tail wrapped securely around him, sound asleep.

He hopped out of his little lair, making the rounds and checking on all his friends. Frowning, he wondered what had awakened him ... everyone slept with contentment. He hopped over to the caribou, who watched him.

"Why do you wander about, Heathcliff? The guards are posted. Use this time to rest so you'll be refreshed for the next watch."

"I heard old Rasputin. He's been howling throughout the night." Heathcliff scratched his long floppy ear. "It woke me twice, did you hear it?"

"I did. I heard some cries into the night, but unlike Rasputin's, I would know his piercing howls, sadistic and laughing at us all. This was a call for help, almost a sad wailing, certainly not befitting the mean old Rasputin that we know."

"But ... but what does it mean?" stammered Heathcliff.

"The less you worry, the better! We have a situation here that needs our undivided attention; probably some poor little victim Rasputin has cornered. Go back to your lair. Morning will be kinder to us all."

The caribou turned back to her turning of the herbs, putting more on to bring Sasha's fever down.

Heathcliff hopped back, checking once more on all his friends, all curled up with their families and fast asleep. Before entering his own lair he looked again at Mr. Mouse, sleeping sound as a babe. Sighing, he crawled back into his little bed and stared out into blackness, wide awake and apprehensive.

■■

Mr. Owl watched Rasputin all the way from his trek towards the retreat, witnessing his capture of the little black wolf pup. He sadly saw the little pup run for cover into the dense brush. Sadly also he had witnessed the little one's ancestors shot by poachers a week ago.

There was only so much he could do. It was the way of the forest ... to live one day carefree and happy, the next second alone and trying to survive. He sighed. If he could save the forest, he would, from all the pain and struggles. His little friends had to learn to outsmart and build up their survival skills to protect themselves. During the day is when such shootings happened. He was useless during the daylight hours – all owls were. By the time night fell he witnessed the daytime cruelty, and all too late to do anything. He hoped the little wolf pup would make it, but he had to do it on his own. Tis the way it is. He didn't make the rules.

Hearing Rasputin stalking the forest last night, he gave up on the little pup. He was a goner. No one ran and escaped from *his* angry jowls. He remembered watching from this tree,

Rasputin sniffing the brush the pup had hidden in. He knew it was a matter of seconds before he was killed.

Curious, and not wanting to flee, he watched. He waited. He stood guard so that old Rasputin didn't enter the retreat where the little cub was being tended to. Surprised, eyes wide in shock, he watched Rasputin with the pup. He flew closer, as quiet as he could, surprised at witnessing the gentle side of the brute.

He didn't know why Rasputin didn't chew him to pieces; he only knew what his big eyes saw – Rasputin was grieving. He wailed high into the night, full of sorrow and disgrace.

He followed them throughout the night, seeing the river scene as Rasputin drunk heavily, then spilled water on the pup, nuzzling into his face gently. He stayed to watch the wolf pup come to life, horror in his little face as he looked into Rasputin's large eyes. He watched, hardly breathing as the little pup challenged the mean old wolf, still barely moving and weak as a newborn calf. What was so unbelievable to Mr. Owl was the fact that Rasputin was tender to the pup; he backed away from him, gentle and as loving as a newfound lamb.

The owl hardly breathed. Then what transpired the next minute was a story to be told throughout the forest for centuries to come ... the wolf pup growled, facing the eyes of old Rasputin, challenging him to attack. Rasputin slowly backed away, placating the little pup with soft growls. Having used all the small bit of energy he had left, the little pup fell down, his last breath challenging the big wolf he had heard of from those

who feared him and warned them all as little as they were ...
stay away from old Rasputin, the evil killer!

Mr. Owl blinked, sadness covering his eyes like a wet
blanket of mist. He blinked again, not believing what he was
witnessing ... Rasputin slowly walking back over to the furry
pup, nudging his leg gently. Not getting a response, he nipped

 his ear as
before – still
no response.
Desperate,
Rasputin
nipped harder
on the ear –
nothing.

Raising his large head, his mane thick with perspiration and
twigs from the forest, he let out a howl that rocked the trees,
filled with mourning and regret.

Mr.Owl watched sadly. Rasputin gripped the pup by the
scruff of the neck and sorrowfully walked back into the forest.
He followed, seeing the wolf head towards the steam coming
out from Sasha's retreat.

The Pact

Rasputin walked into the clearing, seeing the caribou tending to the bed where all the steam had been coming from. The moon shone brightly. Rasputin looked around, seeing no one but the caribou ... and Heathcliff wide-eyed, half out of his lair, staring at the wolf, teeth chattering.

Rasputin growled.

The caribou turned around, staring at Rasputin, scraggly and holding the wolf pup by the neck. The caribou froze, peat moss in her mouth, ready to add to the old.

Wolf and caribou eyed one another.

Heathcliff jumped up, hopping over to Mr. Mouse. The whole camp came wide awake. Scamperings and low, frightened cries echoed throughout the retreat.

The caribou spoke, never taking her eyes off the wolf and pup.

"Listen everyone. Take your young ones and leave as fast as you can."

Everyone gathered their belongings, staring at the wolf.

"But ..." Heathcliff stammered.

"Now," the caribou ordered.

"W-we are n-not leaving without S-Sasha!" Mr. Mouse stuttered, eyes wide with fear.

Mr. Possum tugged at Mr. Mouse's tail, "Listen to the caribou. She'll see that no harm comes to Sasha."

They slowly came closer to old Rasputin, safety in numbers. Rasputin glared at them, gently lowering the pup to the soft ground. He bared his fangs, growling a death-like warning.

All the animals jumped back, looking in the eyes of death and sadness.

"Go now," the caribou repeated. "At least hide in the safety of the deep brush. I will handle this."

Now wolf and caribou were alone. They held eye contact. The caribou watched Rasputin pick the pup up again, crouching closer to the bed of herbs where Sasha lie, belly close to the ground, firmly with hold of the pup's neck. He eyed the caribou.

"What do you want?" the caribou asked. "Why have you come here, carrying a pup?"

Rasputin stretched out on the ground, growling a grief that sliced through the night. He held the black furry pup close to his neck, his large paws holding him close. Head down, nuzzled into the still body, he looked upwards with more sadness and regret than the caribou had ever seen.

The practitioner applied the peat moss to the steam, then took a step towards Rasputin.

Rasputin showed his fangs with a low angry growl, as he dared the deer to come any closer ... he'd attack.

The caribou stopped.

"What is it you want?" she asked again. She eyed the pup. "Is your friend dead?"

Strange sounds came from Rasputin, as though his heart had broken. He rested his furry mane against the little one he held so tightly. All the animals large and small stared in disbelief at what they were seeing, safely hidden in the heavy brush piles they scrambled into.

"I can't help him if you won't let me come closer. Do you bring him for me to make him well?"

Rasputin stared at the caribou, then softly answered with a nod of his head, eyes red from sadness and exhaustion.

"I will tend to your pup if I have your word not to attack any of the creatures here. Do I have your word?"

The wolf answered with another growl, his paws tightly around the pup.

The caribou approached. "You gave me your word. I am a practitioner. If you hurt one of these creatures here at any time I am tending to your pup, I will not help him."

The wolf nodded, looking down at the pup, licking his face gently.

"Let me have a look – I won't hurt him, I must examine him. Once I have established what's wrong with him, I'll do all I can to make him well."

Rasputin released his strong hold, carefully watching the caribou.

The caribou poked gently around the pup, careful not to hurt him. Looking into the weary eyes of Rasputin, she nodded.

"Bring him over to the steaming bed of pines. When you get there stay back a ways. I am tending another."

Rasputin picked his pup up by the neck once more, carrying him to the bed of peat moss. He fell to the ground, still holding on to his pup, stretching out wearily.

The caribou studied them both.

Rasputin sniffed the scent he hated.

Wild eyed, his growls reverberated throughout the area. He looked over where the bed of peat moss lie steaming.

Seeing the bear cub's head uncovered, he bared his teeth, ready to pounce on the sleeping one.

The caribou stepped between the bear and Rasputin.

"If you make one move, I will not help the pup and he will die."

Rasputin glared at the cub, fangs bared in anger. The little wolf pup gave a soft yelp, trying to get away. The wolf broke his gaze from the cub, nuzzling into the little pup. It opened its eyes again, staring into Rasputin's. Both sizing the other up, Rasputin gently licked his face again, trying to still the fear he saw etched on his face. He studied the brilliant yellow eyes of the young one, almost seeing his own reflection.

The caribou waited. All the others hidden in the thick overgrowth stared out in horror, afraid Sasha would be attacked. Mr. Owl stayed transfixed, watching this scene below, happy for once that Daisy was busy preparing her nest for their birthing and new family, and not here with him.

Wolf and caribou stared each other down. The baby pup finally nuzzled deep into Rasputin, making soft suckling sounds, trying to find a teat. Rasputin flung his large paw around the little head searching for milk. He glared up at the healer, still growling, deep and menacing.

"He will die without the proper nourishment. He needs milk. I can get that for him, but not before we have an agreement: I save your pup, and you leave Sasha alone, and all the other creatures here in this retreat."

"Keep the runt away from me! Keep all the mangy furballs at a distance. If any of them come close to me and this one, I will kill them all!" he snarled.

The little pup jumped, trying to break free once more from the gruff sounding giant. Rasputin stroked the little head, making soft, gentle sounds to comfort the frightened one. He felt the relaxed body snuggle back into him, and dug deeper into his side, seeking milk.

"A deal then. You're not known to keep your word, but you appear to have taken a liking to the pup. How did you come by it? Did you kill the ancestors?"

"No!" Rasputin snarled. "I heard something in the brush! I went after it, and came out with this pup, one of my kind. I didn't see the ancestors. You save him, and I will keep to my promise to let all these mangy curs live! If the pup dies I will destroy every one of you!"

"Hmmp," the caribou grunted, "still making threats. Well, let's give it a try. Leave the pup and go bring back some food. From the looks, this one hasn't eaten in a while."

Rasputin growled.

"He'll be safe. Go. You have my word I will do all I can to heal him."

Rasputin looked towards the brush.

"They will keep their distance, now go."

Rasputin slowly got up, taking the pup by the neck and walking over to the caribou. Gently, he laid the pup down at her feet, nuzzling into the furry little head, leaving his scent on him. He glared at the bear lying on the bed of moss. Baring his fangs, he looked back at the caribou, then the pup, all wet and soft as a bed of dandelions.

"You promised. You have given your word. What's it going to be?" the caribou asked.

Rasputin raised his large head, howling into the wind as he slowly entered the forest in search of food for the little whelp.

To be continued ...

Author's Words

I am a new author. Frustrated at trying to make a living as a voice-over actress, I decided to pursue a hidden dream I have had since a child – To Write! A couple of years ago, I tapped into those desires and my heart and mind reached forth together to find the solace and satisfaction to my being that I crave and need.

Up in the mountains, surrounded by trees and peaks hovering high above me, I hike, I snowshoe, and I track the mountain lion – breathing the same air as they, communicating and appreciating their greatness. Animals have fed me with spiritual food all of my life that has filled me with adventure and purity of mind, body, and spirit.

I live in the Susannah Pass Mountains, in West Hills, CA. with my two feline friends – "Heathcliff" and "Rasputin." My goals are to continue writing and to keep involved with saving the wolf and other wildlife from the human threats of greedy corporations and politicians...to help preserve the land they need - to help in making sure the balance is kept between man and beast.

Jennifer Miller is the author of:
Novel 1 – "Sweet Revenge"
Novel 2 – "Marooned"
Novel 3 – "Autumn Run" (unfinished)
Novels 4,5,& 6 – "Run, Rasputin Run!" Books I, II, & III

ISBN 141208494-6